"Wow!"  her. Hey, Ne

The girl t— ..., brown hair over her ....o walked toward us. She had a yellow-and-white designer scarf draped loosely over a simple cotton dress. Everything about her was neat and elegant.

"Yes, I'm Nell," she said. "Who are you?"

My heart dropped into my sneakers. This was no curly-haired little kid. Nell was fourteen and drop-dead stunning.

"Hello," I said. "I'm Dani. And this is Richie."

"Where's my father?" she asked.

"Parking the car. He'll meet us at the baggage area," I explained.

Nell walked side by side with Richie down the corridor, leaving me tagging behind. Who was the stepsister here? This was *my* hometown and Richie was *my* friend.

"Has anyone ever told you that you look a lot like Tom Cruise?" she asked him.

"Oh, barf," I mumbled.

"What, Dani?" Nell asked.

"Oh, I just said 'nice scarf.'"

One Sister To Many!

by Carol Perry

cover illustration
by Richard Kriegler

*For Victoria Corris
of Dunchurch, Ontario, Canada—
my number-one fan*

Second printing by Willowisp Press 1998.

Published by PAGES Publishing Group
801 94th Avenue North, St. Petersburg, Florida 33702

Printed in the United States of America

Willowisp Press®

2 4 6 8 10 9 7 5 3

ISBN 0-87406-903-3

chapter One

"DANI Evans, you are the luckiest four-teen-year-old in Florida," Sara said. She stood in the middle of my bedroom, looking at all of my things. "Just look at this place! The furniture! The curtains! The lamps! Everything is gorgeous, except . . ."

Sara frowned suddenly. She'd been my best friend since third grade, but I couldn't always figure out what she was thinking.

"Except what?" I asked.

"Except for that mutt!" Sara said, pointing to my dog Mickey as he scampered through the doorway. His long skinny tail wagged happily. "He just doesn't blend in very well with your new bedroom."

Mickey looked up, wagged his tail, and then lay down on the fluffy white carpet between the twin beds. I leaned over and scratched his scruffy gray hair behind his ears.

"I guess not, but I love him anyway," I said. "And that's what's important."

"I know," Sara agreed. "I hope Mickey realizes how lucky he is."

I nodded as I turned down my new blue-and-white flowered bedspread. "Yeah, if Doc Sam hadn't rescued him and given him to me, he would've been put to sleep. It's hard to think about that."

"Yeah, it was sad that Mickey's old family couldn't keep him, but it turned out great for both of you," Sara said. "Doc Sam sure is a nice man."

Sara was right about that. Doc Sam is a great guy, a super veterinarian, and a wonderful stepdad. I lost my real dad when I was five and I don't remember him very well. Doc Sam and my mom get along so well together that it seems as if we've always been together.

"He's so handsome," Sara said with a deep sigh. "Tell me again about how your mom and Sam found each other again after being apart for years. It's the most romantic story I've ever heard."

I smiled as I slid into my bed and pulled up the covers. Sara couldn't get enough of mushy love stories. She read romance books all the time. Every time Sara slept over at my house I had to tell her the story of how my mom and stepdad got together.

"Okay, but this is the last time," I said as I clicked off the light.

"Grumble, grumble," Sara said and giggled.

"Back when my mom was in high school, she and Doc Sam dated each other," I began.

"And they always said that when they grew up they were going to get married," Sara interrupted.

"Who's telling this story?" I demanded.

"Sorry," Sara said. "I just don't want you to leave out any of the good parts."

"Well, Mom was really pretty and Doc Sam was very handsome," I continued, thinking of Mom's picture in her yearbook. Even though it had been a long time ago, her blond hair had been styled a lot like mine was now. "They dated all through high school, but then after they graduated . . ."

"They drifted apart," Sara said dramatically.

"Because they went to different colleges," I added.

"And they lost touch with each other . . ." Sara said with a sigh.

"And married other people," I said. "Mom married my dad and Doc Sam married . . ."

"Lauren Lake!" Sara practically screamed. "He married a real-live, famous movie star!"

"She wasn't famous then," I reminded

Sara. "Anyway, back when they were in school, Mom and Doc Sam—"

"He wasn't a vet yet," Sara pointed out.

"I know that!"

"Tell it right," Sara said. "Your mom and Sam . . ."

"She wasn't my mom then, either, since you're being picky," I said. "She was just Jean."

"Okay. You win," Sara said, grinning.

"While Sam and Jean dated, they talked about getting married and having kids. They both wanted a baby girl that they'd name Danielle," I said.

"And even though they didn't marry each other, they each had a girl they named Danielle," Sara said for me.

"Yes." I nodded in the darkness.

"Your dad died. Sam and Lauren Lake got a divorce. And when Sam and Jean saw each other at their high school reunion, sparks flew all over the place," Sara said, falling back against her pillow with a huge sigh.

"And then they got married," I said. "The end," I added with a sigh.

"Are you nervous about tomorrow, Dani?" Sara asked suddenly. "I mean, won't it be weird to meet your stepsister—the *other* Danielle?"

"Yeah," I admitted. "I'm a little nervous. I don't know much about her, except that she probably lives this totally glamorous life. And she probably knows all kinds of famous kids. But I'm excited that I sort of have a sister and she's fourteen, just like we are."

"What has Doc Sam told you about her?" Sara asked.

"I don't think he's seen her very much since she and her mom moved to California. She visits him for a couple weeks a year, but that's it," I said. "At least this time her mom will be busy making a movie in Africa for a while, so Doc Sam and Nell will have a real chance to get to know each other."

"It's lucky that you two have different nicknames or things could get pretty confusing," Sara said.

"Yeah. What if we're both in Mrs. McPherson's class?" I asked. Mrs. McPherson was our English teacher. She hated nicknames and refused to use them. She would call both of us Danielle.

"I think that would be great," Sara said between giggles. "No one will know who she's talking to."

"I wonder what Nell will think of our school," I said, picking up my teddy bear from the floor and hugging him.

9

"We'll find out soon," Sara said.

"Hey, do you want to come to the airport with us to pick her up?" I asked.

"I'm baby-sitting," Sara reminded me. "But I'll come over afterward to meet her—and to see if she looks like a movie star's daughter."

"The only picture of Nell I've seen is the one Doc Sam carries in his wallet. It was taken when she was about six," I said.

A few minutes later, both Sara and Mickey were snoring softly. But I was still wide awake. I really wanted to like Nell. I knew that Doc Sam wanted us to get along and be like real sisters. I couldn't tell him that I was afraid he'd forget all about me once his precious little Nell moved in with us.

My real dad had died in a plane crash when I was only five. I only remember a few things about him, like the time he took me for a pony ride at the zoo. And I loved the piggyback rides he gave me. I still missed him, but I liked having Doc Sam in our lives now. He was funny and smart. And he loved animals so much.

*   *   *   *   *

On Saturday morning, Sara left early to go baby-sitting. I dressed in my favorite jeans and the yellow sweater Mom gave me for

Christmas. Mom says that yellow looks good with my brown eyes and blond hair.

"Ready, Dani?" Doc Sam called from the bottom of the stairs.

"Yep, I'm on my way," I called back.

"Come on, Mickey," I urged my sleeping dog. "Let's get some breakfast."

Mickey stretched and trotted down the stairs behind me.

Mom was happily fixing breakfast. She was enjoying being home for a change. She had worked for a long time as a clothing buyer at a local department store. Now she stayed home and took care of the new house and Doc Sam and me.

"Are you sure you don't want to go along to the airport?" Doc Sam asked Mom.

"Yeah, I don't want to overwhelm her," Mom said. "I'll see her when you get home."

"What's the big deal? She's not coming to stay forever, Mom," I reminded her.

"I know," Mom said, "but I'd like her to feel welcome. I'd like her to visit us as often as she can."

"Is Richie going, too?" I asked.

"Yeah, he just went to check in on the animals," Doc Sam said. "We can pick him up on the way out."

Richie and I had been buddies since we

were in kindergarten. He helped Doc Sam out around the office. He was a great friend. I could tell him anything and he'd understand. Sara said that Richie really hung around to be near me, but I told her she was crazy.

Doc Sam and I jumped into the jeep, waved good-bye to Mom, and drove down the driveway toward his animal hospital and boarding kennel. His office was at the end of our winding driveway near the main road.

Doc Sam blew the horn as we pulled up beside the kennel. Richie raced out and jumped in beside me.

"Hi," he said cheerfully.

"Hi. How are the animals?" I asked.

"Happy enough," he said, his blue eyes twinkling.

We talked about the animals most of the way to the airport. We hit a traffic jam on the Tampa Bay bridge and pulled up to the terminal five minutes before Nell's plane was scheduled to arrive.

"She'll be at Gate C-40," Doc Sam said as he stopped the car near the entrance. "I called the airport earlier to find out. You two go meet her. I'll catch up with you at the baggage claim."

"How are we going to recognize her?" Richie asked me as we headed through the doorway.

I shrugged. "I guess we just look for a four-teen-year-old girl who looks like either Lauren Lake or Doc Sam. We'd better hurry. Her plane should be landing."

We found the right gate and headed toward the line of passengers coming off Nell's plane.

"Is that her?" Richie whispered loudly as a little kid with pigtails walked by us.

"Of course not!" I said. "Nell is fourteen."

"How about that one?" he asked, pointing to a chubby girl with glasses. Even though I knew there was no way Lauren Lake would have a daughter who looked like that, I wished it were Nell.

"No way," I said.

Then I saw a strange look come over Richie's face.

"Wow," he mumbled. "That must be her. Hey, Nell!"

The girl tossed her long, smooth, brown hair over her shoulder and walked toward us. She had a yellow-and-white designer scarf draped loosely over a simple cotton dress. Diamond studs sparkled in her ears. Everything about her was neat and elegant. Even her finger-nails were perfectly manicured.

"Yes, I'm Nell," she said. "Who are you?"

My heart dropped into my sneakers. This

was no curly-haired little kid. Nell was fourteen and drop-dead stunning.

"Hello," I said. "I'm Dani. And this is Richie."

"Where's my father?" Nell demanded.

"He's parking the car," I explained. "He'll meet us at the baggage area."

Richie just stood there with a goofy look on his face.

"Well, at least my father showed up this time," Nell said, handing her gorgeous white eelskin case to Richie. "You know, the name Richie really doesn't suit you. I think I'll call you Rick."

Nell walked side by side with Richie down the corridor and onto the escalator. They left me tagging along behind them. Who was the stepsister here? This was my hometown and Richie was my friend. Suddenly I felt like a fifth wheel.

"Rick, has anyone ever told you that you look a lot like Tom Cruise?" Nell asked.

"Oh, barf," I mumbled.

"What, Dani?" she asked. "Did you say something?"

"Oh, I just said 'nice scarf.'"

14

chapter TWO

IT was easy to spot Nell's luggage coming off the conveyor belt. There were four white suitcases that matched her carry-on bag. I tried to imagine how all those clothes were going to squeeze into my closet. I had cleared a lot of my clothes out and put them in boxes, but I hadn't expected Nell to bring enough stuff to fill a whole store.

Just as Richie made a leap toward the revolving carousel to grab one of Nell's suitcases, Doc Sam spotted us and waved.

"Oh, Nell! It's great to see you!" he said, grasping his daughter in a tight hug.

"Hi, Daddy," Nell said softly, almost sounding shy. I looked at her closely. Who was she trying to kid with her sweet act? A few minutes ago she was bossing Richie and me around like we were little kids.

"I guess you've met Dani," Doc Sam said.

"I'm so glad to have both of my girls together."

"Yeah, it's great," I agreed, forcing my voice to sound more enthusiastic than I felt.

"How many suitcases did you bring, anyway?" Richie interrupted.

"Oh, I don't know," Nell murmured. "Here are my claim checks." She produced a stapled-together stack of little ticket stubs.

Doc Sam took the stubs from her and soon accounted for all her luggage.

"Maybe we should get one of those luggage carts," I suggested.

"Good idea," Doc Sam said. "Let's go find one, Richie."

Seconds later, I was alone with Nell. She stood there and stared at me. She didn't say a word. I looked back at her, noticing for the first time how much she looked like her dad.

Maybe she's just nervous about traveling so far from home, I thought. After all, she doesn't even know her own father very well. It would be rough to go to a strange city and see your dad living with a new family. She's probably worried that we won't like her. Or that we don't want her to stay with us.

"How was your plane ride?" I asked, suddenly feeling a little warmer toward my new stepsister. "I've never been on a long plane trip like that."

16

"It was okay." Nell inspected her manicure. "I'd already seen the movie though."

"You must see tons of movies!" I said, instantly thinking how stupid that sounded. Of course Nell saw lots of movies. Her mother was an actress—and a star.

Nell just looked bored. She nodded and then turned to watch Richie as he pulled the luggage cart toward us. He and Doc Sam struggled to fit it all on the cart. As soon as they put the last one on top, another slipped off. They finally gave up and each carried one.

Richie wasn't watching where he was going and smacked into a garbage can.

"Hey! Watch where you're going!" Nell commanded.

Richie looked at her with surprise. "Are you talking to me?" he asked.

"I'm sorry, Rick," she said. "But one of my bags has a lot of breakable stuff in it." Then she smiled sweetly at him.

"Perhaps you'd better carry the one with the breakables, Nell," Doc Sam suggested.

"Did you bring everything you own?" Richie teased her.

Nell's sweet smile disappeared in a flash.

"No, I didn't," she replied sharply. "My mom suggested I bring lots of clothes because she had no idea how long I'd be forced to stay

17

here. What's the matter? Isn't there room for a few outfits in my closet?"

I noticed a hurt look on Richie's face. I figured I'd better step in and say something.

"Nell, we have a big, walk-in closet," I spoke up. "I've cleared out half of it so you can hang up your stuff."

"You mean we both have to use the same closet?" Nell asked me, like I'd just come up with the weirdest idea in the world.

"Sure," I said. "You're sharing my room. It'll be fun."

"That'll be nice," she said and smiled.

It was going to take me a while to figure out what Nell was really like. I could tell that already.

We headed outside and into the parking garage. After a minute, Doc Sam stopped.

"Why don't you guys wait here while I get the car?" he said. "That makes a lot more sense than pushing all this luggage around."

Doc Sam hurried off, leaving Richie, Nell, and me standing there in the Tampa sunshine.

"Have you ever been to Florida before, Nell?" I asked.

"Nope," she answered bluntly.

"You'll like it here," I said. "It's always sunny and we have Walt Disney World."

"It's sunny in California, too. And we have

18

Disneyland," Nell informed me.

"Oh, yeah. Right," I said, trying hard to think of something clever to say to her.

"Will you be going to our school?" Richie asked finally.

"Yeah, my mom doesn't want me to miss out on school while she's gone," Nell said.

"I can't believe your mom is in Africa," Richie said. "That's so cool."

Nell shrugged. "Africa's okay. I've been there before."

"You have?" I asked, sounding more impressed than I meant to.

"Traveling is no big deal," Nell said. "My mom has dragged me along with her since I was a little kid. She usually tries to schedule roles during the summer so I don't have to miss much school. But this time she didn't have a choice."

Doc Sam pulled the car up to the curb and quickly hopped out. Richie loaded the luggage into the trunk. Some of the pieces had to be jammed in the backseat. Nell slipped into the front seat beside Doc Sam. She seemed to be making herself right at home.

"What is your school like, Nell?" I asked as soon as we were on the road heading home.

Before she could answer, Doc Sam interrupted her.

"You two could probably get some tips from Nell about studying," he said proudly. "Her mom sent me a copy of her latest report card." He beamed happily in Nell's direction.

I sighed. That's all I needed—a stepsister who was pretty, famous, and smart.

"I hope I won't get behind in my school-work while I'm here," Nell said.

"Gulf Beach is a great school," I said a little defensively.

"Oh, I guess it really doesn't matter," Nell said. "I'll only be here for a month or so. Mom can always hire a private tutor for me when I get home."

Nell was making our school seem like a one-room shack. I rolled my eyes at Richie and made a face. But he wasn't even looking at me. He was sitting there, staring at Nell like a puppy dog that was begging for its dinner.

Doc Sam and Nell and Richie—or Rick as they were both calling him now—talked all the way home. I sat there quietly and stared at the passing scenery. I couldn't think of anything to say. I didn't even care anymore what Nell's school in California was like. She'd probably forgotten all about my question. Or maybe she was ignoring me.

I guess it really didn't matter. Nobody was paying attention to me anyway.

chapter Three

MOM was going all out to make Nell feel welcome. She tried to make supper that night into a party. She set the table in the dining room with our best china and crystal and served her famous roast beef.

Doc Sam invited both Richie and Sara to stay for dinner. Sara had been waiting for us when we got home from the airport. She had come straight to our house after she'd finished baby-sitting. I knew that Sara was dying to hear all about Hollywood and the famous kids Nell knew.

Nell sat at the head of the table, the place of honor in our house.

"What a terrific meal," Nell said as she helped herself to a second piece of roast beef. "You're a great cook, Mrs. Parker."

Mom beamed. "I hope you saved room for dessert. We're having strawberry shortcake."

"Of course," Nell said and smiled.

I watched as Nell finished her meal and then dove into her dessert. It was amazing to watch her eat. She ate like a horse and still was as thin as a model. I glanced at Sara to exchange disgusted looks, but no such luck. Sara looked as hypnotized as Richie did.

"It's great to see a girl who isn't afraid to enjoy food," Doc Sam spoke up, looking approvingly at Nell's empty plate.

I gulped a small bite of my shortcake. I've always had a small appetite. It wasn't like I had any choice about it.

Nell talked all through dinner, telling stories about meeting celebrities and their kids. I noticed that everyone seemed to be completely fascinated by whatever Nell said. Was I the only one who wasn't completely starstruck?

When we'd finished eating, I got up and started to clear the table. Sara jumped up to help me. Nell didn't even blink. She kept talking and laughing. I knew she was a guest and all, but for some reason I felt like Nell's maid. And I didn't like that one bit. I dropped the dishes in the sink with a loud clank.

"Hey, be careful," Sara said. "Your mom won't be very happy if you smash up her best dishes."

"I know," I muttered. "I'm just not used to waiting on the star of the year."

"Are you jealous, Dani?" Sara asked.

"No, I'm not jealous," I whispered. "I don't like Nell coming in here and thinking that we should all wait on her. And she's decided that Richie should be called *Rick* now. Isn't that gross?"

"Yeah, it is, but I think you're pretty lucky to have Nell for a sister," Sara said. "She's really interesting."

Then, suddenly, I felt really embarrassed.

"I didn't mean to make it sound like I don't like her," I blurted out. "I guess I just have to get to know her better."

"Yeah, I understand," Sara agreed. "Come on. Let's finish up so we can hear some more of Nell's stories."

"Right," I said as I put in the last dish and pushed the start button on the dishwasher.

Then Sara and I headed back into the dining room. No one was there. I heard music coming from the living room. We saw that Nell was playing the piano and everyone was gathered around her.

She sure liked a lot of attention. I guess I'd just have to get used to it. After Nell played a few more songs, Sara and Richie decided it was time to go home. I was kind of glad to have some time alone with my new step-sister. And I couldn't wait to show off my bedroom to her. I'd finally finished decorating it just the way I wanted.

As soon as Sara and Richie left, Doc Sam carried the last of Nell's bags up to my room. We followed him up the stairs. Everything was exactly in place—everything, that is, except for the heap of bags piled in one corner. I had white wicker furniture upholstered with blue-and-white flowered fabric.

I'd emptied out one of my wicker dressers for Nell to use. I had even cleared off the top in case Nell had pictures or knickknacks that she wanted to put there. On my dresser, I'd placed my favorite ceramic bear, the one Richie had given to me for Christmas. Beside it was the little trophy I'd won for baton twirling when I was ten and a framed picture of my dad.

"Well, this is it," I said to Nell. Doc Sam plopped down the last suitcase and left us alone. "Those are your drawers and I've cleared out half of the closet for you."

"What is *that*?" Nell asked coldly, pointing into the hallway.

"Oh," I laughed. "That's just Mickey. He's a great dog. Doc Sam saved him from being put to sleep."

"What kind of dog is it?" Nell asked, walking backward as Mickey moved toward her.

"Oh, no particular kind," I admitted. "He's very friendly. He won't hurt you."

Nell still looked nervous. "Would you take him downstairs, please?" she asked. "I've never been around animals much. They make me nervous."

The whole thing seemed strange. Her father was a veterinarian and she was scared of dogs. Pretty weird.

"I'll put him out in the hall," I said. "Come on, Mickey. I'm sorry. Give Nell some time to get used to you. Then you can sleep in here again. Okay?"

Mickey sadly plodded into the hallway. Nell sighed with relief as I closed the door behind him.

"Okay, he's gone. Now relax and make yourself at home, Nell," I said.

"This is really a nice room, Dani," she said. She sat in the wicker chair and stretched out her legs. "It's really pretty. Did you pick out the furniture and everything yourself?"

"Yes, I did," I said proudly. "My mom worked in a department store as a decorator for a while. I learned some secrets from her."

"Yes, I really like this," Nell said again as she kicked off her designer sandals. "I had a room almost like it when I was six."

Pow! It felt as if somebody had just kicked me in the stomach. Here she was pretending to compliment my taste. Then—zap, pow— she slipped in an insult as fast and smoothly as she could. How dare she put me down! She didn't even know me yet. I was giving up half my room for her. There were lots of things I'd like to have said to her, but instead I gritted my teeth and smiled.

"Can I help you unpack?" I asked her nicely.

"Would you?" Nell gestured helplessly toward the pile of white bags. "I don't know where to begin. I mean, there's usually some-one around to do it for me."

Was Nell asking me to do all her unpacking for her? I wondered. There was no way that I was going to be Slave Number 3,000 for her. She was going to have to get used to a whole new lifestyle. We lived far from the Holly-wood Hills she was used to.

"I'd be glad to *help* you," I said sweetly. "Besides, I've been dying to get a look at your clothes anyway to see what the girls wear in California."

Nell fished around in her purse and pulled out a key. "Here. This fits all of them," she said. "I'm curious about what clothes I have, too. My mom picks them all out for me."

"What?" I asked her as I twisted the little gold key in the lock. "You have no idea what clothes you brought?"

Nell pulled the lid open on a small suitcase. "Nope," she admitted. "I never know. When I need clothes, my mom calls a few shops and has a bunch of outfits sent over."

"How do you know they'll fit you?" I asked.

"I have one of those dress form things. It's the same size as I am," Nell explained. "It tries on everything for me."

"That's weird," I said.

Nell just shrugged and pulled four silk blouses from her suitcase.

"The dummy can try things on as well as I can. And my mother knows what will look good on me, so what's the big deal?" she asked.

"I guess I think that it's *fun* to pick out clothes," I said. "Don't you ever go shopping with a bunch of friends and try on all kinds of crazy things? It's great for laughs."

Nell didn't answer. I was learning that if Nell didn't want to answer a question, she wouldn't. She'd just pretend that she hadn't heard you. And what was even weirder was that she ignored Doc Sam more than anybody.

"If you brought any pictures or stuffed animals, you can put them over there," I said, pointing toward the empty dresser.

27

"Thanks. I do have a few things I take with me everywhere I go," Nell said, sounding surprisingly sentimental.

For the next hour, Nell and I hung up her clothes in her half of the closet.

"Whew," I said when we'd finished and Nell was arranging more things in her dresser drawers. "I've never seen so many gorgeous clothes in my life!"

"Really?" Nell sounded surprised. "Well, you're welcome to wear anything you like."

"Are you serious?" I asked her. "Really?"

"Sure, Dani. It's no big deal. Help yourself to whatever you like. I mean it."

"Well, gee, thanks, Nell," I stammered, instantly feeling bad for the nasty things I'd thought about her. "And you're welcome to wear my clothes, too."

"Thanks," Nell said as she carried a small, round suitcase over to the dresser.

I plopped down on my bed and watched as she opened it. Everything inside was organized into little tissue-wrapped bundles.

"Need any help with those?" I asked.

Nell shook her head quickly. "No, thanks. I can do the rest."

"Okay," I said. "Well, I'll go take my shower and get ready for bed."

"Uh-huh," said Nell, busily unwrapping the

28

first little bundle.

I grabbed my nightgown and robe from the closet and headed into my bathroom. One of the things I like about my room is having my very own bathroom.

"Your turn," I said ten minutes later as I came back into the bedroom, towel-drying my hair.

Nell was sitting in the wicker chair again, looking at the neat row of little china animals she'd lined up across the top of her dresser.

"Cute," I said. "Do you collect them?"

"Sometimes, I guess," Nell said. "Well, I guess it's my turn for a shower. Now where are my pajamas?"

We both giggled a little, then started a joint search until we found a pair. By the time Nell finished, I had already gotten into bed.

"Dani?" she whispered into the dark. "Are you asleep?"

"Nope," I told her. "Is something wrong?"

"Do you mind . . ." she started softly.

"What, Nell?" I asked.

". . . if I leave the bathroom light on?"

"Sure," I said. "Do you think you're going to wake up and not know where you are?"

"No, that's not it," Nell said. "I'm afraid of the dark."

chapter Four

I was already wide awake by the time Mom tapped on our door the next morning.

"Dani, Nell, it's eight-thirty. Time to get up," she called.

"Thanks, Mom," I answered. I made my way to the bathroom and splashed cold water on my face and brushed my teeth. I felt wide awake.

I looked over at Nell, who still hadn't moved at all. I touched her shoulder.

"Hey, Nell, it's time to get up," I said.

"Go away," Nell answered crossly. "It's the middle of the night."

I laughed. "No, it isn't. Honest. Listen. The birds are singing and the dogs are barking."

It was true. The noisy mockingbird who lived in the old oak tree outside my window was making a racket. And the dogs in the neighborhood sounded like an off-key quartet.

I loved the sounds of morning.

Nell pulled the covers over her head.

"It's morning in Florida," she moaned, "but not in California."

"Do you have what people call jet lag?" I asked.

She groaned again. I didn't know if that meant yes or no.

"Well, whatever it's called, you need to start adjusting," I spoke up. "So let's get going. Breakfast should be ready. And Doc Sam has a great day planned."

Slowly, Nell lowered the blue blanket and peeked out.

"Do you always get up so early on weekends?" she asked as she swung her tanned legs over the side of the bed. "It's not like it's a school day or anything. What's so important that we have to do it now?"

"Doc Sam wanted to show you some of the sights," I explained. "And then we're having a picnic at Fort DeSoto Park. After that, we're going to the bird sanctuary."

"Okay, stop!" She raised her arm in the air. "I know the kind of day my father plans."

Nell hopped out of bed and headed into the bathroom. She didn't seem very happy.

"But he just wanted to show you around," I said defensively.

Either Nell didn't hear me or she pretended that she hadn't heard me.

What's her problem now? I wondered. And then, suddenly, I knew what it was. She was used to a glamorous lifestyle full of excitement. Things that Doc Sam and I liked to do probably seemed pretty dull to Nell.

I pulled on a pair of white shorts and my Georgia Bulldogs T-shirt. I was just tying my tennis shoes when Nell reappeared. She yanked open a drawer, then stared into it.

"I don't have anything to wear," she stated dully.

I couldn't help it. I got the giggles. This girl drags a ton of luggage into my room and says she doesn't have anything to wear.

"I guess you mean you just can't decide what to wear, huh?" I asked finally.

She looked up. "I mean I don't have anything interesting to wear—like what you're wearing."

I looked down at my faded shirt. "Are you kidding?"

"No, all my stuff looks too dressy and formal," she said.

"But, Nell, everyone I know would practically kill for clothes like yours," I said. "You have tons of fabulous shorts and tops."

"I like yours," Nell said again. "I don't have

33

any shirts with sports teams on them."

"Listen, Nell," I said as I began to make my bed. "I told you that you're welcome to wear anything you like." I gestured toward my dresser. "The T-shirts are in the second drawer from the top."

Nell grinned and whipped open the drawer.

"Wow!" she said. "You have tons of great T-shirts."

I gave my bedspread a final pat. "I think you're nuts, Nell," I said, heading for the door. "But if you like my clothes better, go for it. I'll be downstairs."

"Great. And thanks, Dani."

"You're welcome." I closed the door softly behind me, still shaking my head. "Come on, boy," I called to Mickey, who was snoozing at the top of the stairs. "Wake up. It's time for breakfast."

Mickey trotted down the stairs behind me. The aroma of hot blueberry muffins greeted me as I sat down beside Mom at the round kitchen table.

"Good morning, Mom," I said. "Nell should be down in a couple minutes."

"She seems like a sweet girl, don't you think?" Mom asked as she passed me a muffin. "How are you two getting along so far?"

"Oh, okay, I guess," I said. "She's kind of

34

tough to figure out though."

"Give her a little time," Mom suggested. "She is a long way from home. And she's not used to being away from her mother."

"I guess," I said.

"And it's important to Sam that you two like each other," Mom told me.

Just then Nell bounded into the room. She was wearing white shorts and my worn-out University of Tennessee T-shirt. Mom raised her eyebrows a little when she saw Nell wearing my old clothes, but she didn't say anything about it.

Nell slipped into the chair next to mine.

"Breakfast sure smells good, Mrs. Parker," she said.

"Thanks, Nell," Mom said. "Why don't you call me Jean? I think Mrs. Parker sounds a little formal."

I looked at Mom in surprise. She'd never let any of my friends call her by her first name.

"Thanks," said Nell in her sweet, little-girl voice. "I like Jean better. It seems strange to say Mrs. Parker, since that's my last name, too."

"I know," said Mom. "I understand."

Nell looked around the kitchen. "Where's my . . . where's the doctor?"

Where's the doctor? What a weird thing to

call your father! Why was Nell acting like her father was a stranger?

"Doc Sam always gets up early and goes down to the animal hospital to check on his patients," I explained.

"Doesn't he have people who do that for him?" Nell asked in a weird tone. She sounded kind of angry.

"Sure, he has some employees, but he needs to be there, too. He *is* the doctor."

"Well, he's not a *real* doctor," Nell said with a shrug.

Mom and I both stared at her. I couldn't believe my ears.

"Nell," I said. "Do you have any idea how hard it is to be a veterinarian?"

"Nope, I don't know anything about it at all," Nell said as she spread some strawberry preserves on her muffin. "But how hard can it be? They're only animals."

I opened my mouth to defend Doc Sam, but Mom quickly shot me one of her warning looks. Nell quietly ate her muffin and didn't seem to notice that I was ready to explode.

How could she insult her own dad like that? She was lucky that Doc Sam was her father. And somebody should tell her that. I knew I'd better get away from Nell, or I'd be the one to tell her.

"Excuse me, I need to go up to my room for a minute," I said and headed for the stairs.

"Sure, honey. What kind of omelette do you want, Dani?" Mom called after me.

"The muffin was plenty, Mom," I yelled down.

I walked down the hallway toward my room, pounding each footstep as I went. I wanted Nell to know that I was mad. And I wasn't just mad—I was furious.

I kicked open the door to my bedroom. For a second I just stood there and stared. Then I really exploded.

"MOM!" I stood at the head of the stairs and wailed.

"Dani, what's wrong?" Mom asked as she came running.

"Look what she's done," I cried, pointing to my room.

My room looked like a tornado had whirled in, done its damage, and disappeared. And that whirlwind was Nell. There were T-shirts on the beds, on the dressers, and draped over my lampshade. A wet towel lay across Nell's messy bed and her pajamas were on the floor. And her purple passion nail polish was open. I imagined it dripping onto my white carpet.

A minute later, Nell strolled casually up behind us and peered in.

"What were you yelling about? Is something wrong?" Nell asked.

Without saying a word, I pointed. "I don't even want to look at the bathroom," I said angrily. "Just look at the mess you made."

Just then, Doc Sam came bounding up the stairs. "Hey, girls! Good news!" he said cheerfully. "Richie, I mean Rick, is coming with us. Isn't that . . .?" His voice trailed off as he looked from Mom to me to Nell and back.

Mom and I looked sick. And Nell stood there casually munching on a strip of bacon.

"What's going on?" Doc Sam asked. "What's wrong?"

"Oh, Daddy," Nell said in her little-girl voice. "Dani is mad at me."

"Are you, Dani?" Doc Sam asked. "I was hoping that you two girls could get along."

I couldn't answer. I just pointed at the incredible mess that Nell had created. Then I ran into my bathroom as fast as I could and shut the door.

I stood there in the dark and tried not to cry. Why had Doc Sam looked at me like I was the troublemaker? It wasn't fair. Nell turned on her little-girl charm and he fell for it.

After a minute, I flipped on the light. Yep, Nell had trashed the bathroom, too.

chapter Five

I automatically began putting things away. I picked up the fluffy blue towels from the marble top vanity and hung them on the rack.

As I finished wiping away the last trace of Nell's spills, there was a knock at the door.

"Dani?" Nell called through the door. "Dani? Would you open the door?" There was a long pause. "Please?"

"Okay, okay," I said, unlocking the door.

Nell opened the door. We stood in the bathroom doorway and stared at each other.

"You're mad because I made a mess?" Nell asked finally.

"Did you somehow think I'd *like* the mess you made?" I snapped at her. When she didn't say anything, I went on. "How would you like it if I went into your room and threw all your clothes and things around?"

"Dani, I'm sorry I made you so mad," she

said seriously. "I didn't mean to. You could probably trash my room and I wouldn't notice it."

"How could you miss a mess like that?" I wanted to know.

"Because I never have to think about it," Nell said softly. "A couple of maids would run in and fix it back up like new in a few seconds. I guess that sounds kind of strange to you."

"Yeah," I said.

"I'm sorry, Dani," Nell said, staring right at me.

"Well, then, maybe it's time you learned how to do things by yourself," I told her.

"Okay, I'll try," Nell promised.

I walked over to my bed and pushed a few T-shirts out of the way. Nell sat on the other bed, then jumped up when she landed on a wet towel.

"Ewww, gross," she said, then smiled and plopped down again. "I don't clean, but I do lots of other things. I take voice lessons and piano lessons and dancing lessons. I also take tennis lessons . . ."

I stared at her while she went on. I guess I was supposed to be impressed.

". . . and sailing lessons, acting lessons, and bridge lessons," she continued.

"Bridge lessons?" I asked. It sounded pretty

40

boring to me.

Nell nodded. "My mom always tells me how important it is to be well-rounded and have lots of interests. I feel like a spastic yo-yo bouncing back and forth between lessons."

I giggled and pretty soon Nell was laughing, too.

"When do you have time to go out with your friends?" I asked.

"Friends?" Nell asked. "You probably won't be able to understand this, but it's hard for me to make friends. Everybody knows who my mother is and they all want to meet her. I get sick of it."

Nell picked up a Mickey Mouse shirt and tried to fold it. She looked really frustrated and confused. I moved over and sat next to her.

"You really don't know how to fold clothes, do you?" I asked softly.

I thought I saw a tear glistening in her violet-blue eyes. "No, and I feel so stupid."

I patted her arm. "I'll teach you, Nell."

We spent the next half hour folding and stacking shirts.

"There," I said finally. "Now just put all of these T-shirts back where you found them and we'll be all finished."

Nell pulled open one of my dresser drawers

and carefully placed the shirts inside. As she slid the drawer shut, she noticed the picture I had sitting on top of the dresser.

"Is that a picture of your dad?"

"Yes," I said.

"He looks nice," Nell said. "Did . . . did he die a long time ago?"

"Yeah, when I was five," I said. "That's my favorite picture of him, but he was really more handsome than that."

"Why is this your favorite picture?" Nell asked me.

I picked up the frame and looked at my dad's smile. He was wearing a red plaid shirt and an old fishing hat that had a ton of little pins and things stuck in it. He had a little bit of a beard.

"Because it's the way I remember him," I said. I carefully replaced the picture. "Well, tomorrow you're going to learn how to clean a bathroom. I did it for you this time, but don't get used to it."

"Okay," Nell promised. "Let's get going. I'm supposed to be getting the royal tour of the Gulf Beaches, aren't I?"

I gave the room one last glance and we headed downstairs.

"Where's Doc Sam?" I asked when I saw Mom sitting alone in the living room.

"He had an emergency call," Mom said. "Jim Lynch's mare is about to foal. Sam took Richie along. They shouldn't be gone long."

"I just knew it!" Nell burst out. "He does this to me every time."

"Nell, why do you say that?" Mom asked. "Your father is a vet and he has to deal with lots of emergencies, you know. It's part of his job."

Nell didn't answer. She gave us the glassy stare that meant she was tuning us out. I looked at Mom and we both shrugged our shoulders.

"Mom, do you need help packing the picnic basket or anything?" I asked to break the tension.

"No, I think I've got it all ready," she said. "Sara called a little while ago and I invited her to join our picnic. In the meantime, why don't you and Nell go for a walk? You could introduce her to the animals. I think you'd enjoy that, Nell, since you're such an animal lover."

Nell looked surprised. I wondered where Mom had gotten that idea.

"I noticed your collection of miniature animals," Mom explained. "Have you been collecting china animals very long?"

"Uh, yes, I have," Nell said.

"Come on, Nell. I'll show you around," I said.

We headed outside and down the curvy driveway.

"Dani," Nell said uncertainly. "I really don't like animals very much. China ones are okay, but . . ."

"Yeah, I know," I told her. "I saw the way you acted around Mickey. But you may as well see what your dad does for a living."

"Oh, all right." Nell didn't sound very excited about it.

As we headed down the driveway toward Doc Sam's office, I thought about what Nell had said—that he wasn't a real doctor. I decided it was time to set Nell straight about a few things.

"Nell," I began, "about Doc Sam . . ."

"What about him?" Nell snapped. "Are you going to tell me what a great dad he is? That I should be grateful? If you are, don't bother."

I stopped walking and looked at her. "No, I wasn't going to tell you to be grateful. I was going to tell you that he is a real doctor—and a very important one. A lot of people around here depend on your dad to take care of their animals. But now that you mention it, Doc Sam is a great dad, too."

"I wouldn't know!" Nell shouted, putting her hands on her hips.

"Nell, it's not Doc Sam's fault that you and your mother moved to California," I challenged her. "That's thousands of miles from here. He sees you as much as he can and I know that he talks to you every week."

Nell turned away and didn't answer. I didn't know what else to say. Just then, I saw Sara pedaling her way toward us.

"Hi, Sara!" I called.

Sara coasted to a stop next to us.

"Hi, Dani. Hi, Nell. I'm glad your mom invited me to go," Sara said excitedly. "Are Doc Sam and Richie back yet?"

"Not yet," I said. "I was just going to show Nell around the office. Want to come?"

"Sure," Sara answered. She parked her bike next to the sign that said Parker Animal Hospital. "You'll love it, Nell. The puppies are so cute."

"Let's get it over with," Nell grumbled.

Sara looked surprised. I just sighed and pushed open the door that led into the waiting room. Sara walked over to the huge aquarium that practically took up one wall.

"Can you believe all of the fish that Doc Sam has?" Sara asked excitedly.

"My dad takes care of fish, too?" Nell asked.

"Fish are more like a hobby," I told her.

We took a quick tour of the examination rooms, then headed to the kennel area. Sara and I convinced Nell to pet a couple of the puppies. A half hour later we stepped outside into the sunshine. Doc Sam's station wagon was just pulling into the driveway.

"There are my girls!" he called, leaning out the window and grinning at us.

"Hi," Richie said as the car rolled to a stop. "Ready for a busy day?"

"We sure are," Sara said enthusiastically.

"The lunch is all packed," I said.

"How are you, Rick?" Nell asked in a strange tone of voice. It sounded like a smooth, sophisticated voice. Maybe it was one she'd learned in acting class.

Richie fell for it. I could tell by his goofy expression.

"See you up at the house, girls," Doc Sam said and drove on.

I noticed that Nell seemed a lot peppier all of a sudden. She headed toward the house, leaving Sara and me trailing behind.

"What's going on?" Sara whispered. "Isn't that your shirt she's wearing? And what's going on with Richie?"

I kicked a big stone that was sitting in the middle of the driveway. "Yep, it's my shirt. She seems to like my clothes better than her own."

"And what's the deal with Richie?" Sara asked.

"I told Nell to help herself to anything she likes," I said, "and it looks as though she's going to."

chapter Six

NELL managed to push ahead of me and slide in the backseat next to Richie. Mom and Dad were in the front seats. That meant that Sara and I had to sit in the far backseat of the station wagon with the picnic basket and cooler.

"I'm glad you came along, Sara. Or else I'd be pretty lonely back here," I whispered to her.

Right then Richie turned around and looked at us. "Are you two comfortable back there?" he asked.

What do you care if we're comfortable? I wanted to ask him. *You have Nell sitting beside you and she thinks you look like Tom Cruise. Isn't that what's important?*

"Yes, we're fine . . ., Rick," I said.

Sara gave me a funny look.

"Well, he likes when Nell calls him Rick,

49

doesn't he?" I whispered.

"Yeah, but I think he likes lots of other things about Nell, too," Sara whispered to me.

"Who cares?" I snapped, louder than I meant to. Richie and I were just friends. Why was I so upset that he liked Nell?

I looked out the window and tried to concentrate on the scenery. We were on Gulf Boulevard, which runs for miles along the beach on the way to Fort DeSoto Park.

"There's the Sea Bird Sanctuary, Nell," said Doc Sam. "We'll stop there on our way home from the park."

"You'll like it there, Nell," Richie said. "It's one of my favorite places on the beach."

"It is? What's it like?" Nell encouraged him.

Just an hour ago, Sara and I practically had to beg her to look at fish or pet the puppies. Now she was thrilled to hear all about the birds.

"Your dad volunteers there every week," Mom explained. "He helps to take care of any birds that are ill or seriously injured."

"Really? How sweet," Nell said brightly. From where I sat, I couldn't tell if she was being sincere or sarcastic.

I could see Doc Sam's eyes in the mirror, and I could tell that he was smiling by the way they crinkled up in the corners.

It's no wonder he's smiling, I thought. That was the first sort-of nice thing that Nell had said to him since she'd arrived. And she probably only said it so Richie would think she was interested in animals and the bird sanctuary.

"I wonder if there'll be any good shells on the beach," I said, changing the subject.

"There might be," Doc Sam said. "There was a pretty high tide this morning. That usually brings them in."

"I hope so," I said. "I love shelling."

"Me, too," Sara said.

"Shelling?" Nell turned around and looked at me. "How do you do it? Is it a game?"

Nell seemed to think that everything in life required rules or lessons. I couldn't believe she was from California and didn't know what shelling was.

"No, it's not a sport or anything," I explained. "You just wander around and pick up pretty shells. Then you keep the ones you like."

"Oh, that's all?" Nell was silent for a minute. "Is that how you got those big ones on your dresser?"

"Yeah, we found those on Sanibel Island," I said. "That's probably one of the best places to find shells. You can't find anything as good

51

on the beaches around here."

"Remember the morning we found those big shells, Dani?" Doc Sam caught my eye in the rearview mirror. "We both got up as soon as it was light outside and went for a long walk on the beach."

"Yeah, I remember," I said. "It was a lot of fun."

"You'll like it, Nell," Sara said. "Even if the shells aren't huge, it's fun anyway."

"I doubt it, but thanks," Nell said in an icy tone that I wasn't expecting. What had happened to upset her or make her mad? We were just talking and trying to make her feel welcome. Why couldn't she relax and try something new?

I looked at Sara and shrugged my shoulders. Sara rolled her eyes.

When we got to the park, we all helped to unload the station wagon. Sara, Nell, and I carried beach chairs down to the water's edge. Richie carried the cooler that was filled with cans of soda. Doc Sam followed behind us. He carried the picnic basket on one shoulder. Mom walked along closely beside him. She was carrying a big beach blanket.

"They're such a cute couple, Dani," said Sara. "It's great to see your mom so happy."

"Yeah, it is," I said. "They do look good

together, don't they, Nell?"

"Yeah, they do," Nell said. "So, Sara, did you know that if you lightened your hair just a little bit, you'd look exactly like Alicia Silverstone?"

"I would?" Sara asked. "Really? Do you know her?"

"Oh, I've seen her around the studio a few times," Nell explained. "And you do look like her!"

Nell knew just what to say to make people feel good. I glanced at Sara, who was grinning and hanging on to every word Nell was saying. The weird thing, though, was that Nell was right. Sara did look a little like Alicia Silverstone. I'd never noticed it before.

Mom spread out the blanket and we began unpacking the food. Richie sat next to me and Nell and Sara faced us. We munched on Doc Sam's famous barbecued chicken and Mom's potato salad and vegetable curls. For dessert we had three-layer chocolate cake.

"That was fantastic, Jean," Nell said as she attacked her second piece of cake. "You must really love to cook."

"Yeah, I do," Mom admitted. "I'm glad to have more people around to cook for these days."

"Hey, don't I get any credit?" Doc Sam

asked. "I made the most important part of the meal, didn't I?"

Then we all made a fuss over his chicken—everyone, that is, except Nell. She stared intently at her cake and kept eating.

Afterward, we tossed our garbage back into the cooler. Sara and I couldn't wait to get started on our search for shells. We grabbed plastic buckets and headed down the beach.

Mom and Doc Sam sprawled out on the beach blanket, and Richie and Nell ran off to fly an old kite that he'd brought along.

We found a lot of shells and we'd filled our pails halfway by the time we reached the park's famous fort.

"Let's sit in the shade for a few minutes," Sara suggested. "I feel like I'm burning up."

"Sure," I agreed, plopping onto the sand beneath a big palm tree.

I leaned back against the base of the tree and sighed. I'd always loved Fort DeSoto Park. I could remember being at the park with my dad when I was really little. He'd lift me up onto the antique cannon. I had thought my dad was big and strong and the most wonderful person in the whole world. In the middle of my daydream, I caught sight of a colorful kite swooping through the air.

"Richie and Nell are flying that old kite

pretty well," Sara said.

"I . . . I hadn't noticed," I lied.

"Come on, Dani. Tell me what's wrong," Sara said.

"Nothing's wrong," I said quickly.

"Dani, this is Sara you're talking to," she reminded me. "You know you can tell me."

All my feelings suddenly came tumbling out. I told her about the way Nell had messed up my room. I told her how Nell was being so cold to Doc Sam. I even told her how my poor dog was stuck out in the hall all night because Nell didn't like him.

"Oh, Sara, I don't know what to do," I said. "I want for us to get along. Mom told me that Doc Sam wants that so badly. But I just can't figure her out. She can be sweet one minute and mean the next."

I took a deep breath and kept going. "She said I could wear any of her clothes—"

"Whoa!" Sara interrupted. "You're kidding. Nell said you could wear her super-gorgeous clothes? You're so lucky."

"Yeah, Nell was nice about that, but then she blew up at me. She said Doc Sam wasn't a real doctor and she made fun of my taste."

"Are you sure you aren't just being sensitive?" Sara asked. "She sure seems to like your T-shirts . . . and your taste in guys."

"She made fun of my bedroom," I added.

Sara gave me a funny look. "That's weird, because I heard her tell your mom that you have a gorgeous room."

"You did?" I asked. "Well, I guess that proves what I'm saying. There are two sides to her. One is nice and one is mean and grumpy."

"Oh, no!" Sara said. "With two of her and one of you, we now have three Danielles. I think we're in big trouble."

"Very funny," I said with a laugh. "Let's forget it and go look for more shells."

Sara and I walked along with our heads down. I was determined to find one unusual shell to add to my collection.

"Hey, Sara, I think I see—" I said as I ran into something with a thud. "Owww!"

"Hey, watch where you're going," a familiar voice yelled at me.

I looked up and met Richie's eyes.

"Oops, sorry," I said. "Sara and I were looking for shells."

I held out my pail so Richie could see the ones I'd collected.

"Where's Nell?" I asked.

"She's talking to Doc Sam," he said.

"She is?" I was surprised.

"Yeah, he asked if he could talk to her about

something," Richie explained. "I don't know what. Do you want to play Frisbee with me?"

"Sure," I said.

"Hey, Sara," Richie called to her, "do you want to try flying the kite?"

"I'd love to try," she said, taking the wooden block of string from Richie. "Dani, will you take care of my shells?"

"Sure," I answered. I put both buckets of shells out of the way and picked up Richie's Frisbee. I hurled it through the air and Richie jumped up and neatly caught it with one hand. We'd been Frisbee partners for years, so we were a pretty good team.

After a while, we started making more daring throws that challenged our running and leaping abilities. Richie stepped further and further back and threw with all his might. I jumped as high as I could, but the disk went sailing over my head and into a clump of sea oats near where our blanket was.

I finally spotted the Frisbee and headed toward it. ". . . and you didn't even show up for my seventh birthday party!" I heard Nell say.

"But, Nell, there was an airline strike!" Doc Sam explained. "I told you all about that. And I did get there as soon as I could."

"You didn't get there until the next day," Nell cried.

"That's the way things go sometimes, Nell. You're going to have to realize that. And I even took you to Disneyland the next day to make up for it," Doc Sam tried again. "Don't you remember that?"

"Yeah, you take me every place I want to go. You buy me everything I want," Nell said.

"And what's wrong with that?" Doc Sam asked. He sounded confused and I didn't blame him. "I always try to make our times together as fun as possible."

"I know you do. Oh, you just don't see, do you?" Nell sniffled loudly.

"Tell me, Nell," Doc Sam urged her.

"Why don't you ever just take me shelling like you do with Dani? Why don't we ever go on long rides together?" Nell was sobbing. "You just don't like me, do you?"

"Nell, I love you. You're my little girl—"

"No, I'm not a little girl anymore—like that picture you carry around in your wallet. I'm fourteen now. You don't even know me."

Suddenly, I realized I shouldn't be listening. How could I creep away without them seeing me?

"Nell, maybe I haven't been able to be with you as much as I'd like, but I have been there for you," Doc Sam said. "Remember when I used to chase the monsters out of your room every night?"

I grinned, thinking about Nell's fear of the dark.

Nell sniffled, but didn't answer.

"I think what we need is some quality time together, just you and me," Doc Sam said softly. "What do you say, Nell? I'd like for you to get to know your dad better, too."

"What should we do?" Nell asked.

"I know," Doc Sam said cheerfully. "Let's go out for a special dinner tomorrow night."

"Like a date?" Nell asked.

"Yeah," he answered. "And we can talk about anything we want to. It'll be fun."

Just then, I heard Richie yell.

"Dani! What's taking you so long?" he called.

Both Nell and Doc Sam stood up and looked at me.

"Dani," Doc Sam said. "What are you doing there?"

chapter Seven

I tried to think of a good, simple explana-
tion for why I was standing there listening
to their private conversation. I drew a com-
plete blank. Not one smart or witty excuse
popped into my brain.

My face burned and I knew my cheeks were
bright red. I felt stupid and nosy. I decided
I'd better figure out a way to apologize.

"I-I didn't mean to listen," I said, holding
up the Frisbee like it explained everything.

"It's okay, Dani," Doc Sam said. "We're all
family now, aren't we?"

He walked over and put an arm around my
shoulders. I looked into Nell's violet-blue eyes
and saw that she looked really happy. I smiled
and she grinned back.

"Do you mind if we get back to playing
Frisbee?" Richie asked, looking a little uncom-
fortable. "Do you want to join us, Nell?"

She nodded and I tossed the Frisbee in her direction. She caught it and threw a wobbly pass to Richie. He made a nosedive for it and grabbed it. Before long Doc Sam and Mom joined in, too.

We tossed the Frisbee faster and faster until it finally sailed far out of our range.

"Okay, gang, I hate to say it, but we'd better get going if we're going to stop at the bird sanctuary," Dad reminded us.

We all pitched in and cleaned up our mess.

"Here, Nell," I said, handing her a trash bag. "We always walk around and pick up any old cans or bottles or paper that we see."

"But we already picked up our stuff," Nell protested.

"That doesn't matter," I said, pressing the bag firmly into her hand. "Doc Sam says we should always try to leave the outdoors cleaner than the way we found it."

"I guess that is a nice thing to do," Nell said thoughtfully. "I never thought about it before."

She grinned at me and began picking up cigarette butts and gum wrappers that were half-buried in the sand.

"Wow," said Sara. "She looks as though she's shopping for jewelry, not picking up trash!"

"Yeah, I guess it's a new adventure for her," I said.

The ride back up Gulf Boulevard was more fun than the ride down had been. Everyone seemed more relaxed and I liked the new seating arrangement better. Nell sat up front with Doc Sam. Mom and Sara sat behind them. I still rode with the picnic basket and the cooler, but this time Richie sat beside me.

I sneaked a long look at his profile and noticed that Nell was right. Richie did look a little like Tom Cruise. How come I'd never noticed that before? He turned and looked at me, and I could feel the blush spreading across my cheeks like fire.

"Did Doc Sam tell you about the filly he delivered this morning?" he asked.

"I can't believe it," I said. "I forgot to ask him about it. That's not like me at all to forget Doc Sam's patients. Did everything go all right?"

"Yeah, great," Richie said with a big grin. "Doc Sam is absolutely amazing to watch, you know?"

"Yeah, I know."

"I've decided to be a vet, too," Richie said.

"Really? That's great, Richie," I said and meant it. "Doc Sam must be happy about it."

"I haven't told him yet," Richie said. "He'll be even happier when I tell him I want to go to the college where he went."

"Where was that?" I asked. Doc Sam had a plaque hanging in his office, but I couldn't remember what school it said on it.

"The University of Tennessee," Richie said. "It's in the mountains near Knoxville, I think he told me."

Then, suddenly, it all made sense. I should have made the connection earlier. That was why Nell had been searching through all my T-shirts. She'd been looking for a Tennessee shirt to impress her dad.

Doc Sam pulled the station wagon into the driveway of the sanctuary. We all piled out. I had been there a zillion times, but I never got tired of it. There were at least 500 different kinds of birds and most of them were recovering from injuries. Some were so badly hurt that they couldn't fly anymore. The sanctuary gave them a home.

"Here's the brown pelican nursery," Doc Sam said as we stopped in front of a wire-fenced enclosure. He pointed to the big nests of twigs and straw where some of the strange-looking creatures with pouch-like bills sat patiently. "The parent birds are too badly hurt to fly, but the little ones are free to fly away as soon as they're big enough."

"Oh, look!" Nell cried. "That one has only one leg and there is another one with a crippled wing. Poor things. What happened to them?"

"Most of these injuries are caused by people," Doc Sam told her.

"On purpose?" Nell sounded shocked.

"No, not usually," Doc Sam said. "It usually happens when fish hooks or fishing lines get caught on the birds."

"Dani told me that you can cure all kinds of animals," Nell said. "Can't you do something to make them better?"

I noticed that Doc Sam's eyes looked sad.

"I try, Nell," he said softly.

"Your dad spends a full day here each week," Mom said. "He sets broken wings and operates on sick birds and gives injections when they need them. And he's always on call if there's an emergency."

Nell nodded and moved to the next cage.

"This is Gabrielle," Richie said. "Hi there, Gabby!" At the sound of his voice, the reddish bird cocked her head toward us.

"What's the matter with her?" Nell whispered. "She looks okay to me."

"She's blind," I said sadly. "Somebody shot her in the head."

"How terrible!" Nell said.

During the next hour, Nell got a crash course in the four *R*s of treating birds. There was rescue, repair, recuperation, and release. She seemed to be really interested, but then Nell was a good actress. I knew that about her already.

"At least Nell doesn't seem to be afraid of the birds," Sara whispered. I nodded and watched as Doc Sam introduced Nell to the director of the sanctuary.

"Ralph, I'd like you to meet my daughter, Danielle Parker," he said.

I watched as Nell smiled sweetly at him and he commented on how much she looked like Doc Sam.

The words *my daughter* rang in my ears. I knew that I shouldn't be upset by them. After all, she was his daughter—and I wasn't. It bugged me, though, that Nell didn't seem to appreciate her dad very much. If I had a dad, I'd feel like the luckiest girl in the world.

Before I could look away, my eyes filled with tears.

"Is something wrong, Dani?" Mom asked quietly.

I shook my head and tried to smile. "Not really, Mom. I just missed Daddy for a minute. That's all," I told her honestly.

She hugged me. "I do that sometimes, too."

Mom seemed to understand my feelings, because she stayed with me for the rest of

Nell's tour around the sanctuary.

On the way back to the parking lot, we stopped at the little gift shop. Nell spotted a tiny china pelican in the glass case.

"Oh look! It's so cute!" she said, looking at Doc Sam. "Could I?"

"Of course," Doc Sam said and handed her some money.

Then Doc Sam looked toward me like he'd just remembered that I was there. "Oh, Dani, would you like a pelican, too?"

"No, thanks," I said and walked quickly toward the parking lot.

That night after dinner, I watched as Nell happily placed her new little bird with all the other china animal figures.

"He's cute, isn't he?" she asked.

"You seemed to like the birds at the sanctuary," I commented.

"Yes, I really had a good time today," Nell said. She sounded surprised, as if she had expected us to put her through some kind of torture treatment.

"Good," I said. "I hope you'll have just as good a time tomorrow. School, remember? Have you decided what you're going to wear yet?"

Nell looked toward the closet. "I hate picking out clothes. Don't you think it's the worst?" she asked, looking disgusted.

67

"I love picking out clothes," I said. "And if I had your clothes, it'd be great."

"Really?" Nell asked, sounding amazed that anyone could enjoy clothes. "Would you pick out what I should wear? After all, you know what kids wear to your school better than I do."

"Sure," I agreed and immediately began scanning the long row of clothes hanging on Nell's side of the closet.

I checked out everything in her dresser and then began laying out an outfit. I tried different bracelets and scarves with the outfit until I was satisfied.

"You look like a surgeon operating or something," Nell said and giggled. "You're so careful with the clothes. I just toss them everywhere."

"I know," I said and grinned to show her I was teasing.

I picked out a skirt, a brilliantly colored shirt, a scarf, a pair of black shoes, and a matching purse.

"See? It's not so complicated," I said.

"Wow, you're really good, Dani."

"Thanks. When there was just Mom and me, we didn't have money for lots of clothes, so we got creative," I explained. "I enjoyed mixing and matching my stuff."

"Do you want to be a . . ." Nell paused, trying to think of the right word.

"A fashion buyer?" I finished for her. I watched as Nell carefully draped her outfit across the back of one of the wicker chairs. I couldn't believe she was being so neat.

"Maybe," I said. "Or maybe an interior designer. Something to do with fabrics and colors and design."

"It must be a great feeling to know what you want to do already," Nell said.

"What do you mean?" I asked.

"You're really talented at something and you like it well enough to want to do it forever," Nell said.

I thought about that. "Yeah, I guess. You're good at so many things that it must be tough to choose. You could be a singer or an actress or a tennis player," I said, counting on my fingers as I went. "You're so lucky!"

"Me, lucky?" Nell asked, sounding surprised. "You don't understand, Dani. I don't like anything I do and I don't like taking lessons for everything in the world."

"You don't like lessons?" I asked amazed.

"Well, my dad loves taking care of animals. You love clothes and fabrics and all that. I just want one special thing that I do really well. Does that make sense?" Nell asked.

"Even Rick knows that he wants to be a vet."

I felt a stab in my stomach like someone had kicked me. Richie had shared his feelings with Nell, too. I thought that his decision was just between the two of us until he told Doc Sam about it.

"Yeah, he told me about it," I said. "So even though you've had lessons in a zillion things and you've traveled to a zillion places, you've never found anything that you really like to do?"

"Right."

There was a knock at the door. "It's about time for lights out, ladies," called Mom. "Is Mickey going to sleep out here in the hall?"

"Yes," I said.

"No," said Nell. "Please let him in."

I shot her a surprised look.

"I think he'll be happier in here," Nell said and shrugged as Mickey came scampering into the room.

"Good night, Jean," Nell said. "Come on up with me, Mickey."

The little dog snuggled in beside Nell.

"Good night, Danielle and Danielle," Mom said as she closed the door.

Nell reached over and patted Mickey on the head. He looked up at her and gave her hand a friendly lick.

"He likes you," I told her.

"I'm glad," she said.

"Nell, do you want me to turn on the bathroom light?" I asked softly.

"Yeah, if you don't mind," she answered.

I flipped on the switch and crawled under my covers. It would take a while to figure out Nell. That was for sure. But as I drifted off to sleep, I had a warm feeling knowing that I had a stepsister.

chapter Eight

ON school days, I always got up extra early and dressed fast so I'd have time to stop by Doc Sam's office and visit the animals. Richie got there early, too, sometimes. Then we would head for the bus stop together.

This morning I was running kind of late. I gulped down my bowl of cereal and a glass of juice and practically yelled at Nell to move faster. She definitely wasn't a morning person like I was.

We finally made our way down the driveway. I unlocked the door to the animal hospital and yelled for Richie. I'd have to visit with the animals after school instead. Otherwise I'd be late, and I didn't want to get a tardy on my record.

Richie joined us and we walked the couple of blocks to the bus stop. Sara and two other kids were already there waiting for us. By the time the bus arrived, Nell was gabbing and laughing with the two kids like she'd known them forever.

"I've never seen anyone who could make friends so quickly," I whispered to Sara as we took our usual seats. "Look. She's sitting up there next to Tank Tucker. Can you believe it?"

Tank was the best football player on our school's team. And he was handsome, too.

"I've known Tank all my life and he's never sat with me on the bus," Sara complained.

"Yeah. Me, either," I said glumly. It sure was going to be tough having a sister with a superstar personality. "Maybe Tank likes her because she's Lauren Lake's daughter. Some people are like that, you know."

I walked with Nell to her homeroom and stood in the doorway as she made her way toward the teacher's desk. Nearly all the kids stopped talking and looked at her. The room was silent. It was weird and kind of spooky. I guess the news had spread quickly that a movie star's kid would be going to our school.

I waited until Nell's teacher assigned her a seat. There were still a few minutes left until the bell rang, so Nell and I stood out in the hall and went over her schedule.

"I'll see you second period. We're in the

same English class," I told her. "It's with Mrs. McPherson. And we both have early lunch. Sara and Richie do, too."

Nell nodded coolly. "Okay, great. Thanks, Dani. I'll see you second period."

I watched her head into her homeroom. She was as confident as could be. I had to hand it to her. I could never be so relaxed about being dumped in a new school in the middle of the year. She looked beautiful and in control.

I looked down at my own denim skirt and white shirt. I looked okay, but definitely not spectacular. Maybe tomorrow I'd take Nell up on her offer to let me wear some of her clothes.

I slid into my seat just as the bell rang for the last time. I plopped my books onto my desk and looked up into a roomful of staring eyes.

"Is something wrong?" I asked.

"What's she like?" one girl asked.

"Can you get me Lauren Lake's autograph?" another wanted to know.

"Do you think you could get your sister to try out for the class play?" a boy asked.

I just shrugged my shoulders. All anybody wanted to hear about was Nell, Nell, Nell. I was glad when the PA system crackled to life and I was saved from any more questions.

By the time I saw Nell in second period, I realized that I definitely didn't need to help her adjust to being in a new school. I listened as she rattled off three clubs that had invited her to join. She said that she even had a kind-of invitation to the Homecoming Dance.

I did my duty, though, and introduced her politely to Mrs. McPherson. "This is my step-sister, Danielle Parker," I said. "But she goes by Nell."

Mrs. McPherson gave me her you-know-better-than-to-use-a-nickname look. "We do not use nicknames in my class," she said. "You both shall go by Danielle. I can certainly tell you two apart."

"It will be easy to remember you, too, Mrs. McPherson," Nell said softly. "You look so much like Jodi Foster."

By the end of class, I knew that Mrs. McPherson had been right. She knew which Danielle was which. She used her cold, ordinary voice with me. But when Nell asked her a question, Mrs. McPherson was patient and amazingly sweet. This was a Mrs. McPherson none of us had seen before.

The whole day went like that. I heard through the grapevine that Nell amazed Mr. Cassidy, the French teacher, with her fluent, perfectly accented French. And in social studies

Nell gave the class a first-hand report on what it's like in Russia. She'd spent a whole month there with her mother.

Nell sat with Sara and Richie and me at lunch, but we barely got to talk because so many of Nell's new friends stopped by to say hello. Tank Tucker even sat at our table for the first time. By the time we rode home on the bus that afternoon, I felt like Nell knew more kids at Gulf Beach High than I did.

Mom was out when we got home, so Nell and I had the house to ourselves. We changed into shorts and tops and gathered up a few snacks from the kitchen. Then we went out onto the patio where the late afternoon sun was still warm and bright.

"So what do you think of our school?" I asked.

"It's a pretty good school," Nell said as she bit into a fudge brownie. "The language department seems pretty good. I like all the new computers you have and I hear the football team is undefeated."

"Yeah, but what about the kids?" I asked her impatiently. "You sure are popular with them."

Nell took a sip of milk. "Oh, that."

Was I imagining things or did Nell sound bored?

"What do you mean by *oh, that?*" I asked.

"They don't like me," Nell said. "They like who I am—Lauren Lake's daughter—big deal."

"Nell, that's not true. I think they really like you," I explained.

Then I realized that I was being a hypocrite. That morning, I'd agreed with Sara about kids liking Nell for her glittery star status. And now I was telling her that it wasn't true. I guess I really didn't know what to think.

"Oh, I don't mind it," Nell said. "It gets me just about anything I want, except . . ." Her voiced trailed off.

"Except what?" I couldn't believe that there was something Nell wanted and didn't have.

"I'd like for my dad to come home," she said quietly.

I just sat there with my mouth open.

"But Doc Sam *is* home," I blurted out.

"Oh, I know that," Nell said. "I know he's happy with your mom and that my mother loves her work in California. But when I was little . . ."

She stopped talking and looked down as if she was embarrassed to go on.

"Tell me," I urged her.

Her eyes looked sad. "I used to imagine that my dad would come back and that we'd be a real family again."

I nodded sympathetically and took a bite of my brownie.

"But it never happened," Nell said. "I knew it was stupid, but every time he came out to see us, I'd dream that he'd stay and never leave again. I always hoped he and Mom would fall in love all over again."

"You've been hoping that for a long time, huh?" I asked.

"Yeah, it's silly, huh?" Nell asked. "I know he's never going to be my dad again."

"Wrong," I said.

"What do you mean? He stopped being my dad a long time ago," Nell said flatly. "He's your dad now."

"In the first place," I said, "he'll always be your dad. That kind of stuff never changes. It doesn't matter where you both live. And, besides, he never left you."

She didn't say anything to protest, so I went on. "I know what it's like to wish your father would be there forever and ever. I used to wish that my dad would find his way home and that his dying was all a mistake. I'd pretend sometimes that it wasn't my dad who had died in the plane crash. I'd remember how my dad came home after work and hugged me and made me happy. At least your dad is alive."

"Oh, Dani." Nell moved closer to me, and put a comforting arm around my shoulders. "I'm sorry. I didn't think . . ."

"It's okay." I wiped my eyes on my sleeve. "I think you should appreciate Doc Sam because he's always there if you need him and he does care about you."

"I still feel like he deserted mom and me," Nell insisted.

"But it was your mom who left. She wanted to go to California and she took you with her," I pointed out.

"But Mom's career was in California," Nell said defensively. "She didn't have a choice."

"You're not being reasonable about this," I said. "Doc Sam was in vet school when you and your mom moved to California."

"Yeah," Nell said. "But he could have gone to another vet school."

"It's not that easy to get into vet school, you know," I defended Doc Sam. "There aren't that many good vet schools in the country."

"No kidding?" Nell asked, taking a sip of her milk thoughtfully. "I didn't know that."

"You probably should have asked him about it," I said. "Why were you and Doc Sam arguing yesterday?"

"Because he wanted to know why I was acting so cold toward him," Nell admitted. "So

I told him."

"You told him what?"

"About all the times he's put other things before me. I always feel like I'm at the bottom of his list or something," Nell explained. "I get really tired of it."

Could we possibly be talking about the same Doc Sam? I wondered.

"You can't be serious! He visits you in California as much as he can. And he calls you on the phone every week, doesn't he?" I asked.

Then I stopped. "I'm sorry. It's none of my business. Only I think you're too hard on Doc Sam. I really hope you can get things straightened out between you when you go out to dinner tonight."

"Thanks. But it won't be easy," Nell said. "He stood me up so many times for things that meant a lot to me."

"Like your seventh birthday party?" I asked, remembering what I'd overheard.

"Not just that," she said. "Once he was supposed to spend Christmas morning with me and he didn't show up until three o'clock."

"Wait a minute," I said. "Your dad travels thousands of miles to see you and if he's a couple of hours late, you make a big deal out of it?"

"Well, it *was* a big deal," Nell said, pouting. "I was only ten. I cried all morning."

"Did he have a good reason for being late?" I asked her.

"I guess. Something about animals, like always," Nell mumbled.

"You're impossible!" I exploded. "How can you be so selfish? You are so lucky to have a dad, and especially to have Doc Sam for your dad."

When Nell didn't answer, I went on. "And I'm tired of you ignoring me when you don't like what I'm saying."

I stood up and headed for the patio gate. "I'd give anything to have a Christmas afternoon with my dad. Just one afternoon. Any afternoon!"

"Dani?" Nell called after me. But I borrowed one of her tricks. I pretended not to hear her and let the gate slam shut behind me. I took off running down the curved driveway.

chapter Nine

I ran until I reached Doc Sam's office. He was just finishing up his last patient for the day. I stood in front of the big aquarium wall and waited. I pressed my forehead against the cool glass and gazed into the tank.

Brightly colored fish swam lazily past a tiny treasure chest. Feathery green plants grew among the sculptured bridges and caverns that made up the pleasant underwater world. I tried to imagine what it would be like to be a fish. They just swam around and around without a worry in the world.

"Dani, you're just the person I wanted to see!"

I jumped at the sound of Doc Sam's voice. "Hi, Doc Sam," I said. "I was just imagining what it would be like to be a fish."

"Do you do that, too?" Doc Sam asked, smiling.

"Sometimes I wonder what it'd be like to have nothing to do but swim around and look pretty and wait for someone else to clean your tank and feed you."

"I guess it could get boring," he admitted.

"What did you want to see me about?"

"I need to know what my dau—what Nell is planning to wear this evening," he said.

"I don't know. She hasn't said anything about it. Why?" I was curious.

"I'd like to buy her flowers, a corsage, to wear," Doc Sam said with a little grin.

How was I going to ask Nell what she was wearing when I'd just run down the driveway to get away from her? But I couldn't tell Doc Sam that I'd just told his daughter off and that I thought she was a spoiled brat. Besides, he rarely asked me to do anything for him.

"I'll see what I can find out," I said. "Give me a few minutes."

"Thanks, Dani," Doc Sam said.

I headed back up the driveway, prepared to apologize if I had to. Nell wasn't on the patio or in the kitchen. But I noticed that she had cleaned our glasses and plates.

"Nell," I called, poking my head into the living room. "Where are you?" There was no answer. I checked the TV room and the dining room, then headed upstairs.

As I climbed the stairs, I realized that I wasn't mad anymore. Maybe it was from all the running around. Or maybe seeing the proud look on Doc Sam's face when he talked about buying flowers for his daughter had done it. Whatever the reason, I was ready to face Nell—if I could find her.

Then I saw that the bedroom door was closed. "Nell?" I tapped on the door softly. "Are you in there?"

"Yes," she said. "Come in."

Nell lay on her bed, her head resting on Mickey's belly. She was hugging him as though he was her best friend.

"Are you okay, Nell?" I asked. "I'm sorry I yelled at you. It was none of my business anyway." I sat down on my bed.

Nell sat up. "Don't apologize, Dani," she said. "I've been thinking about what you said. You were brave to tell me what you thought. Not many people do that."

"Well, never mind," I told her. "Let's think about what you're going to wear to dinner tonight. You only have a couple of hours to get ready."

"Yeah, I do want to look good," Nell said, standing up and opening the closet. "Will you help me pick out something? I think tonight will be the chance to really tell my dad how I feel about things. I'd like to get to know him better."

Within minutes, her outfit lay across the bed. I'd helped her pick out colorful pants and a cute, white shirt. To go with it, we chose her diamond stud earrings and a small, white purse.

"That's going to be perfect, Nell," I said. "Hang it up carefully. I have to go run a quick errand."

I headed for the doorway.

"Where are you going?" Nell asked.

"Just down the road. I'll be back in a little bit."

"Okay. I'll wash my hair," Nell said. "That'll keep me busy until it's time to get dressed."

"Leave plenty of time to clean up the bathroom, too," I warned, still remembering yesterday's mess.

"I will," Nell promised and smiled.

I hurried back down to Doc Sam's office.

"She's wearing a white shirt," I told him. "So just about any color of flowers would be fine."

"Something pink, then," said Doc Sam. "She always liked pink flowers when she was a little girl."

"Umm . . . Doc Sam," I said. "Maybe you

should pick a different color. You know, to show that you realize she's grown up."

"I guess you're right, Dani," Doc Sam said. "I still see her as a little girl sometimes, but she's really not. What do you think about a corsage of red roses?"

"I think that'd be perfect," I said with a grin.

"Dani, do you have any film in your camera?" he asked me.

"Sure," I told him. "Why?"

"Because I think it's time to take a new picture of Nell to put in my wallet." He opened his wallet and held up the old picture of Nell. "Maybe you could take a picture of the two of us together before we go out."

I knew how Doc Sam felt about that picture of Nell. I felt sentimental, too, about the picture of my dad that I kept on my dresser.

"Doc Sam," I said, "you don't have to get rid of the old picture, you know. Just keep it in a special place, so you can look at it when you want to remember."

Doc Sam looked at me thoughtfully as he slipped the photo out of its plastic sleeve. "You're a very understanding young lady. Do you know that, Dani?" he asked softly, putting the picture carefully into his top desk drawer.

I was embarrassed. "You'd better get going

if you want to get that corsage."

"Look at the time. I'll phone the florist, then drive over and pick it up."

Mom was home when I got back to the house. We decided to fix frozen dinners and watch TV together.

"Seems like old times," she said, ruffling my hair affectionately. "Just you and me having dinner in front of the TV."

"This is great," I said and meant it. Mom and I always had fun together. "I hope Nell and Doc Sam will get to know each other better while she's here."

"Like we do?" Mom asked.

"Yeah, like we do," I agreed, giving her a hug.

When Doc Sam got home, Mom and I were getting ready to eat our dinners. He proudly showed us Nell's rose corsage.

"She'll love it, Sam," Mom said.

It had five roses, some teeny little white flowers, and a silver bow.

"I'd better get changed myself," Doc Sam said, looking at his watch. "Would you tell Nell that I'll be ready in a flash?"

I dashed up the stairs and knocked on the door again. It seemed strange to knock on my own bedroom door.

"Come on in, Dani," Nell called. She really

sounded happy.

"Wow!" I said. "Double wow! You look fantastic." She turned around slowly and her diamond earrings sparkled. "Wait until your dad sees you. Your hair looks so pretty. I wish I could get mine to do something," I complained.

"I know what you mean," Nell said. "I have the same problem with making my hair behave."

"What do you mean?"

"Mom has a special conditioner made up for me. It's amazing," Nell confided. "Go ahead and try it. If you like it, I'll have a big batch sent to you."

I opened the bottle. It smelled like coconuts and almonds. "Thanks," I said. "I'll try it tonight."

"Come on, Nell," I told her. "Let's go downstairs. Doc Sam wants me to take a couple of pictures of you two together."

"He does?"

"Yep. He's decided that he'd like to have a new picture of you two to put in his wallet!"

Nell smiled and opened the bedroom door. "I'm ready. Let's go."

I knew something was wrong as soon as we reached the kitchen. Doc Sam was still in his white lab coat and he was talking on the phone. I looked at Mom questioningly. She put her finger to her lips.

"Shhh," she warned. "It's Ralph from the bird sanctuary. There's been a terrible accident—it's an emergency."

I looked at Nell and watched as her eyes filled with tears.

chapter **Ten**

I watched Doc Sam's face as he talked. From the deep creases in his forehead, I could tell that something was wrong.

He caught my eye and placed his hand over the receiver.

"It's an oil spill in Tampa Bay," he said glumly. "And it sounds like a bad one. There's a lot of work to be done."

I nodded. There had never been an oil spill in the bay, but Doc Sam had prepared us for any kind of disaster.

"Do you want me to round up some of the kids to help?" I asked.

"Yes, Dani." Doc Sam was already on his way out the door. "And ask them to bring old towels and hair dryers if they can."

"We'll find you at the bird sanctuary in a while," Mom said to him. "Dani, why don't you go use the office line to call the kids and I'll use this phone to get a hold of the environmental group volunteers."

"Hey! Wait a minute, Dad," Nell spoke up. "What's going on? What about our dinner?"

"I'm really sorry, sweetheart. You'll have to take a raincheck on dinner. This is a major emergency," Doc Sam said and let the door bang closed behind him.

"You can't do this to me!" Nell yelled. She stormed across the kitchen and opened the door. Doc Sam looked back at her.

"Do what?" Doc Sam asked.

"You promised!" she insisted. "You said you wanted to spend some time with me."

"Nell, this is an emergency. Don't you understand?" he asked. "We'll talk about this later. Right now I've got to get my bag. I don't have any time to debate this."

Nell followed him across the porch. Mom and I stood where we were and listened. "You're standing me up for some dumb birds," she said, raising her voice. "I can't believe it."

There was a moment of silence. And then Doc Sam spoke calmly. "Yes, I am. And you, young lady, need to get your priorities straight. I have to go to the hospital, pick up my bag and some antibiotics, and head to the bird sanctuary. I'll be there until this emergency is under control. If you want to help,

Dani and Jean will tell you how you can. If you don't want to help, fine. But stop acting like a child about this."

I walked over to the doorway. I couldn't see Nell's face but I could see her shoulders shaking. I knew that I should probably try to comfort her. Inside though, I felt the same way Doc Sam did. I knew how excited Nell had been about going to dinner with her dad, but emergencies came out of the blue. And she would have to understand. After all, she wasn't the center of the universe.

I looked back at Mom. Then I slowly closed the door and left Nell standing on the porch alone. I had phone calls to make.

I walked into the den and plopped down at the desk. I called Richie and Sara first. Each agreed to come over and ride to the sanctuary with Mom and me—and Nell if she decided to help us.

I quickly made fifteen more calls and got our group together. All of the kids had worked as volunteers at the sanctuary and had signed on as part of the emergency squad. The squad had never handled anything like this before.

The kids agreed to meet at the beach as fast as they could. As I hung up from my last call, I could hear Mom talking on the kitchen phone.

"Dani, please run upstairs and grab a couple of hair dryers," she called to me.

"Okay, Mom," I said and dashed up the stairs. My bedroom door was shut again. This time I didn't bother knocking. I pushed the door open. "Nell," I ordered, "I need your hair dryer."

Nell was lying face down on her bed. She rolled over slightly to look at me.

"My hair dryer? Why?"

"We use the dryers to warm up the birds after we're done cleaning them. Come on, I've got to hurry," I urged her. "Your dryer is the least you can do."

Nell looked surprised and a little hurt that I was being so harsh with her. But she got to her feet quickly and handed me her hair dryer.

"Here," she said. "Need anything else?"

"No," I told her. I picked up my own dryer and started out the door.

"Dani. Will you wait?" Nell called after me. "I'm coming with you."

I looked at her dressed up in her silk outfit and her fancy white shoes.

"Are you kidding? You're wearing that?" I asked and started to close the door.

"No, really. Wait. I mean it. I am coming."

"Nell," I said as patiently as I could, "I don't have time to wait for you to change. Richie and Sara are on their way over, and Mom's probably already in the car waiting for me."

"I'm coming—in this." Nell sounded very determined.

"Well, at least change your shoes," I told her, heading for the stairs.

When I looked outside, I saw that I was right. Mom was just climbing into the driver's seat. Richie and Sara were already in the back. A few seconds later, Nell and I climbed into the car beside Mom.

"Aren't you a little dressed up for this, Nell?" Sara asked innocently.

Nell didn't answer. Instead, she yanked off her dress shoes and tugged on her black high-top sneakers.

By the time we reached the sanctuary, the parking lot was already full. TV reporters and camera crews were milling around, trying to get the latest news. The cleanup operation definitely was a hot topic. We'd listened to the car radio during the drive over and learned that the spill had been caused by an oil tanker that had run aground.

"Will the oil spread to the beaches?" Nell asked.

"Yes, it will," Mom told her.

As Mom locked the car, the rest of us headed toward the workroom where rows of tubs were lined up on wooden tables. Lots of volunteers, with their sleeves rolled up, dunked birds into the sudsy water.

Two people worked on each bird. Ralph, the sanctuary director, explained what to do during each step of the cleaning process.

"Once a bird is exposed to oil," he said, "a twenty-four-hour clock starts ticking. If a bird hasn't been cleaned and dried by then, we put it to sleep. Otherwise, it will die anyway."

Ralph opened a cage and held out a sickly bird to me. Nell, standing close beside me, took a startled step backward.

"Come on, Nell," I whispered. "I'm holding its wings so it can't get away. Just grab the bird's bill and hold it closed. We'll get it into the tub." Nell looked frightened, but she did exactly as I'd told her.

It was hard to see the oil on the bird's dark feathers, but once the bird was in the tub the messy globs of oil quickly rose to the surface of the water. Sara stood by with a hair dryer, ready to dry the poor thing as quickly as possible.

After the bird was cleaned, Nell wrapped it in a towel and placed it gently on the drying table. Sara carefully aimed the warm air at his freshly washed feathers. Then another team of workers took over. They were in charge of administering special vitamin-packed food to the bird through a feeding tube.

We followed the same process with bird after bird. Every once in a while I'd spot one of my friends through the crowd and wave. But there was no time for talking and fun.

After a while the steady procession of oil-soaked birds in carrying cages stopped piling up.

"There'll be more as soon as morning arrives," Ralph said grimly, "but it's too dark to search for them now. We'll take a boat out at dawn to look around the island areas where the birds nest. Meanwhile," he gestured toward the pile of cages, "we've got more than enough birds here to keep us working through the night."

"Don't the birds know enough to stay away from the oil?" Nell asked. "Oil is so messy and ugly."

"How would they know it's nasty?" I asked her. "No one tells them. They see a calm-looking kind of water. It has a nice, shiny film to it. Birds dive down to check it out and get oil all over them."

"Oil disrupts the feather structure," Ralph explained. "It keeps them from being water-repellent. So if the bird can get out of the water, he'll head for the nearest dry spot and start cleaning off his feathers."

"And he'll end up eating the oil?" Nell asked, making a face.

Ralph nodded. "Then he's got a toxic, poisonous substance on his feathers and inside his belly, too."

"It's the oil on the inside of the birds that finally kills them if we don't clean them fast enough," I explained.

The time passed by quickly. Every once in a while, we'd change jobs with each other. After I'd been washing birds for a long time, a girl came along and took my place at the tub. I moved over to the drying area, where I rubbed the wet birds with soft towels or gently parted and ruffled their feathers while someone else dried them.

At some point, Nell disappeared in the direction of the infirmary, where Doc Sam and members of the sanctuary staff were working to save birds who'd already swallowed the poisonous oil.

As the twilight turned to darkness, Richie and some of the other guys joined us.

"Hi, Dani," Richie said as he grasped a terrified white egret. It struggled as he tried to wash the heavy sludge off its once-white feathers.

"That sure is a wiggly one," I said, stepping

in to help him. "Most of them don't have that much pep."

"I know." Richie agreed. "It's sad."

"Do you know if Doc Sam is saving many of them?" I asked.

He nodded. "Yep. He says that most of the birds we brought in tonight have a pretty good chance. But the ones we find tomorrow won't be so lucky."

"Did you see Nell in there by any chance?" I asked. "I haven't seen her for a while."

"Yeah. She's helping Doc Sam. And naturally Tank is right in there beside her."

"Tank?" I asked. "What's Tank got to do with Nell?"

Richie handed the clean bird to the drying team. "You mean you haven't noticed? I'm surprised at you!" A brief smile flickered across Richie's face. "Tank is crazy about your sister. He even asked her to go to the Homecoming Dance."

"Tank? I doubt if she took his invitation seriously, though," I told him.

"Why?"

"Well, for one thing, she doesn't think anyone really likes her," I explained. "She thinks all the attention she gets is because of her mother."

Richie laughed. I looked up at him, surprised.

"What's funny about that?" I demanded. "I think it's sad."

"It would be if it were true," he said. "But Tank doesn't even know who Lauren Lake is."

"You're kidding," I said doubtfully. "Where has he been?"

"Tank likes adventure movies and that's it," Richie said.

"Does Nell know that?"

"Of course not. I told him the names of a few Lauren Lake movies so he could pretend that he knew about her mom," Richie explained.

"Do him a favor," I suggested. "Tell him to confess the truth. Nell would like him a whole lot more if he did."

"You think so?"

"I'm positive!"

Finally, the endless relay race of birds stopped. "You kids have been a tremendous help," Ralph told us. "But you have school tomorrow. You'd better get home and get some sleep. Doc Sam and the rest of the sanctuary staff will help me take care of things until morning. Maybe by then the spill will be contained."

"Oh, Dani, Richie. There you are." Mom sounded tired. "I've found Sara, but Nell seems to be missing. Do you know where she is?"

"She's in the infirmary, Mrs. Parker," Richie offered.

"She's helping Doc Sam," I added.

"She is?" Mom was surprised, too. "Would you run in and get her, Dani? We're ready to head for home."

"Sure." I walked toward the plain, shingled building that served as the hospital for the birds. I realized that my muscles ached and my clothes and hair smelled like oil.

I reached the door of the hospital and pushed it open. Nell wasn't hard to find. She stood at the front of the room next to Doc Sam. They were surrounded by people from the local TV stations who were covering the cleanup.

Nell held the neck of a Great Blue Heron as Doc Sam gently forced a feeding tube down its throat. Nell's sleeves were rolled up, her long hair pulled back with a rubber band. Her earrings glittered under the hot glare of the TV lights. And somehow, the ridiculous outfit—diamonds, hightops, and filthy black oil—looked good on her.

"Hey, Nell!" called a camera operator. "Over here! How about a big smile?"

Without losing her grip on the bird, Nell obliged. "You must be proud of your daughter," someone said and shoved a microphone in

101

front of Doc Sam. "She's pitched right in to help during this disaster."

"Yes, I am very proud of her," said Doc Sam.

Right then, I felt stupid standing there. I felt like I'd intruded on a second private father-daughter moment. Deep inside me a tiny voice cried out, *What about me?*

But I didn't say anything. I just stood there and watched until the bright camera lights finally dimmed and went out.

chapter Eleven

L OTS of kids needed rides home from the
sanctuary.

"Hey, gang, no problem," Doc Sam said
when he saw the group of kids out front. "I
have to run back to my office to pick up a
portable x-ray machine anyway. I'll take everyone who's headed in that direction."

Mom drove the kids who lived on the other
side of town. Sara, Richie, Nell, and I piled in
with Tank and a couple other kids. Richie
winked at me from the front seat and pointed
discreetly at Tank, who'd wedged himself between Nell and me.

But Nell still didn't seem to be paying
special attention to our high school's football
star. Instead, she leaned back in her seat and
stretched her filthy arms out straight in front
of her. Her usually perfect nails were chipped
and dirty.

"Wasn't that fantastic?" she asked. "Nothing like that has ever happened to me before!"

Nell sounded so sincere. But was she really making fun of us? Life in Hollywood had to be tons more exciting than an oil disaster in Tampa. Or was she talking about being on TV?

"Yeah," I said. "You'll probably be on the news tonight."

Nell looked at me like I was pretty stupid. "I don't care if I'm on TV or not," she said, sounding disgusted. "That's nothing. I've been on TV before."

"Then what—"

"I'm talking about what we all did tonight!" she gushed, breathless.

"Washing dirty birds?" I asked. "You liked it?"

"Well, *like* isn't exactly the right word," Nell said thoughtfully. "After all, the poor things were suffering. But, Dani, I never felt so useful before."

"Well, sure," I said. "We were all useful. That's what being a volunteer is all about."

"But, Dani. Don't you see?" Excitement shone in Nell's eyes. "I've never done anything that was really useful in my whole life."

Tank looked back and forth between Nell and me as we spoke. His head bobbed back and forth like he was watching a tennis match.

Tank said something to Nell in a low voice that I couldn't make out. Soon, Mom stopped the car in front of his house.

"See you at school tomorrow, Nell," Tank said, stepping on my foot as he climbed out the door. "And save me a place beside you at lunch, will you?"

"Yes, Tank. I will. Good night," Nell said.

After Tank left, Nell leaned back in her seat and closed her eyes. I did the same. I barely managed to mumble good night to the other kids as they were dropped off.

A short while later, Doc Sam, Nell, and I stumbled into the kitchen, tired and dirty. Mom joined us a few minutes later.

"Do you have time for a cup of coffee before you go back to the sanctuary?" Mom asked Doc Sam.

"I think I'll take the time," he said, sitting down at the table.

"Wait a minute, before you get comfortable, Doc Sam . . ." I picked up my camera. "Let me get a picture of you and Nell, the way you looked on your date."

Doc Sam laughed and stood up. "Good idea! Come on, Nell," he said. "And by the way . . ." He opened the refrigerator, leaving a black smudge on the door. "I have a surprise for you, honey." He handed Nell the florist's box.

Nell tore the cover off and lifted the roses from their green tissue-paper bed. She breathed the fragrance deeply, then held them out to Doc Sam. "They're beautiful. Will you pin them on for me?"

Doc Sam pinned the silver-trimmed corsage to Nell's ruined shirt. Then they both smiled proudly for the camera.

"Got it!" I said. "That'll sure be a great picture to remember tonight by."

"I don't need anything to remind me of this evening," Nell said. "I'll always remember it."

"Was it that terrible, Nell?" Doc Sam asked with a frown.

"Terrible? Of course not!" Nell whirled around. "That's not what I meant by remembering this evening. I thought the whole thing was wonderful. And you were great, too. It was the best date I've ever had . . . except for one thing."

"What's that?" Doc Sam wanted to know.

"We never had dinner," Nell said. "And I'm starved."

Doc Sam grinned.

"Why don't we all have a snack before we go up to bed?" I suggested.

"Let's get cleaned up first," Mom said. "Then we'll have a late supper . . . or an early breakfast. I hope your teachers will try to understand if you both fall asleep in class tomorrow."

"I've got to get back to work," said Doc Sam. "I'll eat later. Thanks for your help. You all were great."

He kissed Mom lightly, leaving a new smudge on her cheek.

As soon as Doc Sam was gone, we all went to clean up. Nell used the guest bathroom and Mom used the bathroom in her room. In my own bathroom I stood under the hot stream of water in the shower for a long time. I scrubbed oil from beneath my fingernails and from the creases in my hands and arms. I lathered shampoo into my hair over and over again. I reached for conditioner and, remembering Nell's offer, picked up the pink bottle.

Later, clean and in my pajamas, I sat in my pretty blue-and-white chair and combed my hair. Mickey looked up at me, then went back to sleep.

Nell came into the room. "Hey, guess what?"

"What?"

"I even cleaned the guest room tub," she announced. "Sure was a surprising day, huh?"

I smiled. "Let's go downstairs and eat and see if we made the ten o'clock news," I said.

We had. I was surprised to see myself on

TV. Richie and Sara were on screen, too. I'd been so busy I hadn't even noticed the cameras. There was a close-up of Nell holding the Great Blue Heron. The announcer identified her as *the daughter of actress Lauren Lake and prominent area veterinarian, Doctor Sam Parker.* And then the camera went to Doc Sam and his words of praise for his *daughter*.

And again, that tiny voice cried out from deep inside me. I was the Danielle who always made her bed, did the dishes, and helped out with everything. Why was Nell praised for helping out once? Big deal.

I ate the fried egg sandwich Mom put in front of me and drank some hot chocolate. But I barely tasted any of it.

"I'm almost asleep," I announced. "I'm going to bed now. Thanks for the food, Mom. Coming, Nell?"

"Go ahead, Dani," said Nell. "I'd like to talk with Jean for a few minutes."

I yawned and carried my dishes out to the kitchen. I heard Nell's voice as I climbed the stairs heading for bed. She was talking about Tank. Nell was having a mother-daughter talk with my mother. And I didn't like it.

Even though I was mad, I flipped on the bathroom light for Nell before I crawled into bed.

I felt refreshed the next morning. I wasn't

tired at all. I was wearing one of Nell's outfits and my hair looked better, too. Nell had
been right about her conditioner.

Sara couldn't get over it. She kept telling
me I looked fantastic. Nell said so, too. Richie
seemed to approve, because he kept looking
at me.

The bus arrived and we took our usual
seats. It didn't take long for everybody to
make a fuss about us being on TV. They said
it was on morning TV, too. We were celebrities. I liked the feeling.

A couple of kids told us that there had been
good news about the oil spill. The Coast
Guard had worked through the night and the
spill was under control. Lots of birds would
still need to be cleaned up and treated and the
beaches would be yucky for a while. But
things certainly were looking up.

"Sara," I said during the few minutes before
homeroom started. "I just don't know how to
explain it. One minute, I think Nell is great
and the next minute I can't stand her. What's
the matter with me?"

"Nothing," said Sara. "You sound like
normal sisters to me."

"We do?"

"Sure," Sara said, slamming her locker shut.
"I can't stand my sisters sometimes. I think

109

you're supposed to. Usually I like them okay. But if either of them had clothes like Nell's I'd like them even more."

"I know what you mean." I smiled. "I like this part of it," I admitted, looking down at Nell's clothes. "I guess Nell's not so bad for a sister, huh?"

"Bad?" Sara looked surprised. "I think she's fabulous! Everyone likes her."

"Right," I said, slamming my locker door a little harder than I needed to.

Nell's popularity, it seemed, had grown since yesterday. When Mrs. McPherson, who'd seen Nell on TV, asked her to give a brief oral report about caring for the birds, Nell stood up and gave a talk that sounded like she'd been caring for birds all her life. Even I was impressed.

"Thank you, Danielle Parker." Mrs. McPherson beamed her approval.

I didn't see Nell again until lunch. By then her circle of friends seemed to have grown even more. And, of course, Tank sat beside her. He looked as if he were in heaven. Richie sat on her other side. And my best friend sat across from her, hanging on to every word she said.

"Barf," I muttered. I'd almost reached the table when I realized that there wasn't even a seat left there for me. I turned away and slammed my tray down on a table in the corner of the cafeteria. I nibbled around the edges of my over-cooked pizza and forced myself to smile brightly at the guy sitting across from me. I vaguely remembered seeing him in my last year's algebra class.

"Hi," I said, trying to sound friendly, the way I'd heard Nell talk to guys.

I wanted to look like I was having a good time—just in case any of my friends looked in my direction. The guy I was smiling at smiled back. He looked kind of flustered.

"Well, I've got to go. See you," he said a little while later.

I sneaked a glance over at the gang. If anyone had noticed that I was missing from my usual spot, they sure didn't show it. I watched their faces and listened to their laughter. Finally I dumped my half-eaten pizza into the trash and left the room. Right then I wished I'd never heard the name Danielle Parker.

I had promised to help out at the sanctuary again after school. I'd have to go home and change out of Nell's clothes before I went over to help with the birds. As soon as the last bell rang, I raced to catch the first bus. I usually took the second bus, but I just didn't feel like riding with Nell and her fan club.

I got off the bus alone and hurried home. I paused when I reached the animal hospital. I decided that if I stopped and watched the fish for a few minutes, my attitude might improve.

I opened the door to the waiting room and walked closer to the aquarium.

"You know, you guys are a lot like Nell," I whispered. "There'll always be someone around to clean your tank and bring you your favorite food." The fish swam around and ignored me. "That's okay. My best friends don't notice me anymore either. Why should you?"

I pressed my head against the tank and watched as my breath made a little steamy spot on the clean glass. I jumped when I heard a phone ring. I could hear Doc Sam's voice on the other side of the wall.

"You've got it?" Doc Sam said. He seemed pleased. "And it's eighteen-karat gold?"

I knew he wouldn't buy gold for his animals. It had to be for Nell. No doubt. Or maybe it was for Mom. Yeah, that was more like it.

"Okay," Doc Sam continued. "Here's the inscription I want to have engraved on it. Ready?"

Here I was again, listening to a conversation that was none of my business. I knew I should leave. But I couldn't get my feet to listen. I pressed my ear right up to the glass.

"For my dear daughter, Danielle Parker," said Doc Sam. "With love and pride, Dad."

I bit my lip. For acting like a human being once in her life, Nell was going to get a gold bracelet, a reward for helping. I slipped quietly out the door and ran toward the house. It wasn't fair.

Nell was already home when I got to the back door. Through the screen door, I could hear Mom talking to her in the kitchen.

"I know how much you love chocolate cake, Nell," Mom was saying. "So I have one in the oven now."

"Thanks, Jean." I knew without seeing her face that Nell was all smiles and dimples. "I just love your cooking! I'm going to ask Dad for a ride over to the sanctuary as soon as I change, but I'd like a big piece of cake when I get back."

"Fine," said Mom. "Where's Dani? Isn't she with you?"

"Nope," said Nell. "I think she took the early bus."

"Oh, then I guess she's at Sara's," Mom said.

"No," Nell said, "Sara sat with me on the bus. Well, I have to go upstairs and change. Come on, Mickey."

The familiar click of Mickey's toenails on the tile floor meant that he'd obeyed her. Great. Nell had not only taken over my closet, my bathroom, my best friend, and Richie, but she was taking over my mother and my dog, too.

"Hi! I'm home!" I yelled, deliberately letting the kitchen door bang shut behind me.

And I hoped with all my heart that I'd slammed it hard enough to make that stupid chocolate cake fall flat.

chapter Twelve

I barely spoke to Nell as I changed my clothes. She tried to start a conversation, but I either gave her one-word answers or pretended not to hear her.

Mom drove us over to the sanctuary. I chattered on about school stuff, trying to make myself feel better before we got there. Nell sat in the backseat, looking out the window. The news reporters had said the crisis was under control, but it sure didn't look that way when we got there.

The oil-soaked birds were sitting in carrying cases waiting to be cleaned. Most of them looked even worse than the birds we'd helped the night before.

Nell and I were assigned to work side by side. I knew that Sara, Richie, and Tank were somewhere around, but I couldn't see them from where we were. It didn't matter. Helping the birds was the most important thing.

I even began to feel ashamed of myself for being jealous of Nell.

"How could an oil spill like this happen?" I asked angrily. With each bird I cleaned, I got madder. "How could anyone be so stupid to dump black slime into our Gulf?"

"Doc Sam said it was caused by a misunderstanding," Nell spoke up. "He said a worker on the tanker ended up running it aground. Then the tanker got a hole in it and spilled out the oil. It's so sad."

"You'd think people would listen and try to understand each other better, wouldn't you?" I asked as I sprayed warm rinse water onto the bird's feathers.

"You'd think so," Nell agreed. She carefully turned the bird so that I could reach its dirty tummy.

"You know, Nell," I said, "you're really good at handling the birds. It looks like you've been doing this for years."

"Really?" Nell asked, looking up at me. "Thanks, Dani. I just hope we've been able to help save some of them."

"Me, too. If this was a small oil spill, can you imagine what would happen if there was a big spill?" I asked. I reached into the next carrier and pulled out a sad-looking pelican.

"This guy didn't get it too bad."

Nell took the pelican and stroked its feathers softly. It seemed to relax a little.

"Look at that," I said. "He seems to understand you. I've seen Doc Sam do that lots of times."

"Do what?"

"Communicate with the animals he's working with. He calms them right down," I explained, "just like you did."

"No kidding?" Nell's eyes twinkled. "Dani, do you think this is something I might be good at?"

"Are you nuts?" I asked her. Was Nell blind or what? "You're good at everything! Why would you be surprised that you're good with birds, too?"

"I'm not good at everything, Dani," Nell said defensively. "And, besides, I want to be good at something important, something that really matters."

She fluffed the pelican's feathers affectionately, then handed it over to the drying crew.

"It's just that I've never . . . oh, forget it. You wouldn't understand," Nell said, letting her voice trail off.

"Nell, try me. Just because we're from different backgrounds doesn't mean I won't understand," I said.

117

As I said that, I realized that that was true. Nell sure could make me mad, but I did care about what she was thinking and feeling.

Ralph came along just then and suggested we take a break. "It's going to be another long evening, girls," he said. "But I'm happy to say that all the publicity on the news helped a lot. We had a lot more volunteers show up today. Why don't you two take a walk for ten minutes or so?"

Gratefully, we agreed. We washed our hands, then walked toward the water's edge. There was no sign of oil on the beach yet.

"Maybe the oil won't get this far," Nell said, reading my mind.

"I sure hope not," I agreed. "I heard the tanker was only half full."

"Dani, do you think my father likes me?" Nell asked out of the blue.

I was so surprised by her question that I couldn't answer for a minute. I looked at her, trying to decide if she was serious.

"What do you mean?" I asked. "Of course he likes you! He's always bragging about all the stuff you do. You play the piano. You're a great tennis player. You're—" I stopped because I knew I sounded jealous.

"But, Dani, that's not what I mean," Nell said. "I want him to really like me—as much as he likes you."

"Me?" I didn't know what she meant. Yes, Doc Sam liked me. We had a lot in common. But I wasn't his daughter. He didn't like me in the same way he liked Nell. He loved her.

"Yes, you," Nell said. "He's always saying how great you are. He says how responsible you are. You're good at everything that I'm not."

Nell looked so sad right then that I forgot about being jealous of her looks and the way people fell all over her.

"Is that why you're so excited about helping out here?" I asked her.

"It started out that way," Nell admitted. "I wanted to help out because I knew it was really important to my dad. He was really mad at me for being upset that the birds ruined our date."

I nodded. I was beginning to understand where Nell was coming from.

Nell took a deep breath then continued talking. "I wanted us to have something in common—the way you do with him. But after I started helping with the birds, I found I really liked it. They're so little and fragile and they need our help."

"Like father, like daughter," I said and grinned.

She smiled back at me.

Suddenly Nell stopped walking. "I want him to think I'm important," she said softly. "I was mad at him for a long time. When I was little, I felt like he'd left us. I tried to tell myself that I didn't care about him. But I do. I love him. And I miss him."

"Yeah," I said. "I felt that way when my dad wasn't there for me anymore."

"Your dad?" Nell asked, sounding surprised. "But your dad didn't go away. He died."

"But when you're little . . ." I repeated her words.

"So, you do understand."

"Yes, I do," I told her. "And you know what? I happen to know that Doc Sam is super proud of you for helping out here." I thought about the bracelet he was having engraved for her. "I can't tell you exactly what I mean. But you'll find out soon enough. Trust me."

I pushed my feelings of jealousy deep down.

"I do trust you, Dani." Nell was smiling again. "It's funny. Sometimes I feel so close to you. And other times . . ." She made a face.

"You can't stand me?" I laughed. "Or maybe you'd like to trade me for a gerbil?"

"Well, I don't know if I'd go that far," Nell said, giggling.

I nodded. "Sara told me that feeling that way means we're like real sisters."

"Really? I'm so glad!" Nell said enthusiastically. "I thought it was just me."

We walked along the beach quietly. I finally worked up the nerve to ask her. "Nell, what do I do that drives you crazy?"

She looked into my eyes and grinned. "You're too perfect. It's hard to be around you sometimes."

"Me, perfect?"

"Yep," Nell said. "Let's see. You know how to clean, iron, and shop. Everyone likes you. Your mom and my dad are so proud of you. You have great friends like Sara and Rick. And you don't even have to buy them stuff or get them autographs."

"Nell, I wish you'd stop saying that people only like you because your mother's famous. Don't you know that some of the kids have never even heard of Lauren Lake? And one of those kids is Tank."

"No way," Nell said.

"If your mom played for a pro football team, he might be impressed," I told her. "But I don't think he knows anything about movie stars."

"But he knew the names of two of her movies," Nell said.

"That's because Richie coached him," I confided. "Richie told me that last night."

Nell's smile broadened. "That's great," she said happily. "He really likes *me!*"

"That's what I've been trying to tell you. Well, I guess we'd better get back to work," I announced.

"In just a minute," Nell said. "Now it's my turn. What do I do that drives you crazy?"

"Nothing much," I said, trying to find a way out of this.

"Come on, Dani. I told you."

"Okay, okay. But I don't want to hurt your feelings," I said honestly.

"I understand that. So just tell me," Nell said impatiently.

"Well . . ." I began. Then I stopped. I couldn't think of one important thing that bothered me. Nell's messiness drove me bonkers at first, but she'd been doing a lot better. I couldn't tell her that all her gorgeous clothes made me super jealous. After all, she said I could borrow them any time I wanted. And there was no way to say that I felt sick when I saw her confiding secrets to my mother—or that I didn't like her calling Richie *Rick*.

"Hey! There you are!" Richie called out just then. "We've been looking for you."

I waved in his direction. "Hey yourself.

What's the matter? Who's looking for us?"

"Me. Sara. Tank," Richie said. "But especially me." He smiled and the corners of his blue eyes crinkled up. He fell into step between Nell and me as we walked toward the wooden boardwalk that led from the beach to the bird sanctuary. "I haven't seen much of you lately, Dani. Is something wrong?"

"What do you mean?" I asked.

"You didn't sit with us at lunch," he explained, "and then you ducked out on us after school."

"Oh, that." I could feel my face growing pink.

"We thought . . . Sara thought . . . you might be upset about something," Richie said.

"No, I'm fine," I said, plastering a phony smile on my face.

"If you say so," Richie said. He didn't return my smile. "Maybe you should let Sara know everything's okay. See you around." He turned abruptly and walked away.

"What was that all about?" I wondered aloud.

"I think it was about that guy you ate lunch with," Nell spoke up.

"I didn't think he even noticed."

"Yes, he noticed. He hardly ate any of his lunch," Nell said. "Wouldn't you be a teensy bit jealous if he ate lunch with another girl?"

"But he did . . . I mean, the table was full. I mean, I didn't even know that guy, Nell," I confessed. "I was just acting kind of weird, I guess."

"Maybe you'd better explain all that to Rick," Nell urged.

She was right. Richie and I were good friends. I didn't want to ruin that. I had to do something to clear up the mess I'd created—and fast.

"Thanks, Nell," I said and ran toward the sanctuary.

chapter **Thirteen**

I burst through the doors of the sanctuary, ready to tell Richie the truth. But as I walked into the treatment area, I saw that he was already busy. He was holding down a bird while Doc Sam gave it a shot of antibiotics. I'd have to talk to him later.

I quietly took my place again at the bird-washing table. The time flew by. We all cheered a couple of hours later when we saw that the cages were all empty.

"Let's clean up here," I suggested to Nell, "then we'll go find the others."

We emptied our tub, scrubbed the table-top, and tossed the dirty towels into a big hamper. I tried not to look at the row of metal cans that held the birds that hadn't survived the oil spill.

"Well, that's it," said Nell, giving the wooden table a final swipe with a cleaning rag.

"Let's go find the gang."

"Right," I said. "I want to clear up things with Sara and Richie."

"Good," Nell agreed. "Here they come now."

I looked over to see Sara, Richie, Tank, and Doc Sam walking toward us. They all looked tired, too.

"Hi," I said when they were close enough to hear me. "You guys all finished?"

"Yep, we are," Doc Sam said. "There's not much else you kids can do. But you've all been really great. You should be proud of yourselves. Together, we've saved lots of birds."

"Uh, Dani, Doc Sam has invited us to your house tonight for ice cream and cake," Sara said.

"You kids deserve a celebration," he said cheerfully. "Besides, Dani's mom just made one of her great chocolate cakes."

"It'll be fun," Nell piped up. "Maybe we could rent a movie to watch."

"It's okay with you, isn't it, Dani?" Sara sounded anxious. "You don't mind if we come over, do you?" She looked down at her dirt-streaked sweatshirt. "After we get cleaned up, I mean."

"Of course it's okay." I smiled at Sara. "I'm sorry if I acted a little weird today. I'll explain everything later."

Sara looked relieved that I wasn't mad. Richie did, too. Tank just looked at Nell as usual. But this time I saw that she looked back at him the same way.

"Well, then," Doc Sam said. "It's settled. I'll drive everyone home and you can all come over later for dessert."

We headed for the station wagon. I still hadn't had a minute alone to talk to Richie. But I was determined to find a way to get my message across while we ate dessert.

As soon as we got home, I raced for the bathroom. I let the hot water splash over me and thought about what an amazing day it had been. I finished my shampoo with a big blob of Nell's conditioner, then wrapped myself in my fluffy bathrobe. I opened the door to the bedroom and saw that Nell was already there towel-drying her hair.

"Have I told you how much I like your room?" she asked.

Not exactly, I thought, thinking back to her crack about my room looking childish.

"No," I said. "I don't think so."

Nell looked puzzled. "I had a pretty room like this when I was about six. It was blue and white and ruffly. I loved it. Of course, my room wasn't as sophisticated as yours is."

"Really? You think my room is sophistcated?"

I asked to be sure I heard her right.

"Yeah, it is," Nell said.

I'd spent so much time being mad at her. And I'd misunderstood what she had been saying.

Nell sat down in front of the dressing table and began combing her hair. I opened the closet door and stared at the row of clothes on my side. I wanted to look really nice. I finally picked my best jeans. But I couldn't decide which top to wear.

I held a white sweater in front of me and looked into the mirror. Then I tried a pink blouse. "Which looks better, Nell?"

"I don't know much about coordinating clothes," Nell said. "But I think you should wear my silky top."

"Really? Thanks," I said as I slipped it over my head. It looked great on me.

"Nell, I want you to know that you don't have to lend me your clothes for me to like you," I said.

"I know, Dani," Nell said softly. "I really do know that now. Thanks for saying it, though."

"Sure," I said. "Are you almost ready to go downstairs?"

Before she could answer, there was a knock at the door.

"May I come in for a minute?" Doc Sam called.

"Sure," I said.

He opened the door and peeked in.

"I wanted to thank you two again for all you did to help the last two days," he said, walking over beside the dresser. "I'm proud of both of you."

Just then, his sleeve brushed against a china giraffe and knocked it on its side. "Oops, sorry." He set the little figure upright, then stared at it for a moment. "Nell, didn't I buy that for you at the Los Angeles Zoo?"

Nell didn't answer. Instead, she looked down at her hands.

"And this one," Doc Sam said, picking up a rabbit. "I remember now. You couldn't have been very old."

Nell nodded. "That was the first one," she said. "You gave it to me on Easter before you and Mom . . ."

"Got divorced," Doc Sam finished for her. "Yes, and I remember this little guy, too." He held up an elephant. "It's from San Francisco." He looked back and forth between the dresser and Nell. "And this one?"

His voice sounded funny all of a sudden.

"You gave them all to me," Nell said.

It seemed strange that Doc Sam had given her the whole collection but didn't seem to remember it very well.

As if reading my thoughts, Doc Sam said, "How could I have been so blind not to notice these? You must think you have a pretty dumb dad."

Nell smiled up at him. "It's not your fault. You buy me so many things whenever we're together. There's no reason you should remember china animals."

"I'll notice from now on," Doc Sam promised, picking up a little horse. "I didn't even know you liked animals."

"I liked that they reminded me of you," Nell admitted softly.

Even though I was sitting in my own bedroom, I felt like I was intruding again.

"You may not be that crazy about animals, Nell," I spoke up, "but we know firsthand that you do like birds!"

"Dani's right," Doc Sam said.

"Yeah," said Nell. "I'm not happy that the disaster happened. But it did teach me a lot about myself."

"That's good, honey. Well, I guess I'd better let you finish getting ready for supper," Doc Sam said. "Oh, by the way, Nell, I have a surprise for you that has to do with birds."

"What is it?" Nell squealed excitedly.

"You'll find out later," Doc Sam said. "See you downstairs."

130

Nell made guesses about the surprise all during dinner. Doc Sam grinned and shook his head each time.

"Aren't you curious about what it is, Dani?" he asked.

I shrugged my shoulders. I already knew that Doc Sam had a special engraved gift for Nell. But I couldn't admit that I knew that.

"Oh, sure," I said.

Dinner was over soon enough. Doc Sam tapped his spoon against his water glass. "Okay, gang, I'd like everyone's attention."

I swallowed hard, willing myself not to be jealous of Nell. After all, she was Doc Sam's real daughter. I wasn't.

"I have some good news for Nell," Doc Sam announced, his eyes shining.

I pasted the phony smile on my face again and waited.

"Ralph from the bird sanctuary had a great idea and he wanted me to find out what you thought of it," Doc Sam said.

What did Ralph have to do with engraved jewelry?

"Ralph?" Nell asked.

"Ralph?" I echoed.

"Yes, he was impressed by how well you handled the birds, Nell. "He thinks you have a special talent for working with sea birds."

"He does? Really?" Nell was excited.

"Tell Nell Ralph's idea," Mom urged.

"All right," Doc Sam promised. "Ralph wants to offer you a job during your summer vacation."

"A job? Me?" Nell stammered.

"It's up to you," Mom said. "You don't have to. I've already asked your mom about it. She said it's fine if you'd like to come back here for the summer. And we'd love to have you here. Wouldn't we, Dani?"

"Sure," I said.

"I'd love to come back," Nell announced. "But a job! I don't know. I've never had a job before."

"You can do it," I assured her. It seemed strange to be encouraging her. Before I'd have been jealous. But I guess I felt kind of responsible for her learning to take charge and help the animals.

"It won't be anything difficult, Nell. And it certainly isn't glamorous," Doc Sam warned her. "You'll be cleaning cages and feeding birds."

"But it's a beginning," Nell said.

"Yeah, that's a good way to look at it," Doc Sam said and smiled.

Nell suddenly dashed around the table and gave him a big hug. "Oh, thank you, Daddy!"

she said in a little-girl voice. "I love you!"

It was a happy moment for them, but I felt like a dam of tears inside me was ready to burst loose.

"May I please be excused?" I asked.

Without waiting for an answer, I ran out of the room and up the stairs.

chapter Fourteen

I threw myself across my bed, warm tears spotting the blue-and-white spread. I felt like a jerk. And even worse, I didn't know exactly why I felt so miserable.

I was happy that Ralph had noticed Nell's work with the birds. I mean, I wish he'd offered me a job, too. But I could probably get one if I asked for it. And I was glad that Nell would be coming back next summer. Above all, it was great that she'd finally admitted out loud that she loved her dad.

I sat up and reached for a tissue from the box on the nightstand. I dabbed at my eyes. I looked up at my dad's face, smiling at me from the silver frame on the dresser.

"Oh, Daddy," I whispered. "What's wrong with me?"

There was a knock on my door a minute later. I dried my eyes.

"Dani? Can I come in?" Doc Sam asked.

"Y-yes," I hiccuped. "Come in."

"Are you okay?" He crossed the room and placed a cool hand on my forehead. "Are you feeling sick?"

"No, I'm not sick," I assured him. "I just felt kind of funny for a minute." I tried to smile. "I'm fine now."

"Are you sure?"

I nodded.

"Are you and Nell getting along?" Doc Sam asked.

"Sure," I said. "We get along fine." I touched the soft collar of her blouse. "We even wear each other's clothes."

"Good. I'm glad you two hit it off. I thought you would," he said.

There was a long silence then. Finally, Doc Sam said, "Dani, there's something serious I'd like to discuss with you."

"With me?" I asked softly.

Doc Sam cleared his throat. He actually seemed nervous. I looked up at him.

"I hadn't really planned to talk about this yet," he said, "but I think maybe this is the right time."

What was going on? I watched as Doc Sam reached into his pocket and pulled out a small, velvet box. "This is for you, Dani," he said.

"It's up to you whether you keep it or not."

I took the smooth, royal blue box from him.

"Maybe I should do this formally." Doc Sam got down on one knee in front of me. "There, that's better." He sounded pleased.

"What's going on?" I asked.

"Dani Evans," he said solemnly, "would you do me the honor of becoming my daughter?"

"Huh?" I asked stupidly, still clutching the box.

"Go on," Doc Sam urged. "Open it. I'm too old to stay bent down like this much longer!"

I took a deep breath and slowly lifted the cover of the box. A gold bracelet shimmered against the blue velvet.

"Read what's engraved on it," Doc Sam said. "I hope you like it."

I already knew what was engraved on it. But I held the bracelet up by its delicate chain links and read the inscription anyway. "For my dear daughter, Danielle Parker, with love and pride, Dad."

"But . . . I don't understand. My name is Danielle Evans. Why are you giving Nell's bracelet to me?"

"Dani, I'd like to legally adopt you. I'd like for you to take my name, so I can really be your father. How does that sound to you?" Doc Sam asked.

I threw myself at him with a big hug. "It sounds perfect!" I said. "Oh, Doc Sam, I'm so happy!"

When I finally let him go, he sat down on the bed beside me. "How about dropping the Doc Sam stuff?" he asked. "I'd prefer Dad."

"Okay, Dad," I said, trying it out. "Would you put my bracelet on for me, Dad?"

As he fastened the golden links of the bracelet, I looked past him at the picture on the dresser. Happy tears blurred my eyes and it seemed—just for an instant—that the smiling man in the old fishing hat winked at me.

"Why don't we go back downstairs?" Doc Sam asked. "We have some news to share."

I grinned. "Okay, let's go." We walked down the hall toward the stairs. I heard voices drifting up from below. "Sara and the guys must be here." I squeezed Doc Sam's arm.

We walked into the dining room. Sara, Tank, and Richie were there with Mom and Nell.

"There you are!" said Sara. "Sit down. It's chocolate cake time."

The cake was on the table, looking fluffy and delicious.

"Hey, Dani. Sit here," Richie said, pulling out a chair for me.

"First, ladies and gentlemen," Doc Sam said seriously, "we have some news for you."

Everyone looked at us and waited. I saw the big smile on Mom's face.

"I'm proud to announce that Dani has agreed to be my daughter—legally, I mean," he said. "She'll soon be Danielle Parker."

I held out my arm so that everyone could see my bracelet. "Look. Isn't it beautiful?"

Naturally, everyone crowded around and wanted to know all the details.

"You and Nell will have the same name?" Tank asked.

"Yep," I said. "Everyone will be confused."

"Old McPherson will have a fit," he said.

I giggled. Then I wondered how Nell was going to feel about the news.

"Nell—" I began.

"I think it's great," she answered before I could get out the words. She gave me a tight hug. "We're really sisters now. I can't believe it."

"You really don't mind?" I looked into her blue eyes, trying to tell whether Nell was acting or telling the truth. "You don't mind sharing Doc Sam with me?"

"Not if you don't mind sharing Jean . . . and Mickey."

"Hey, let's watch a movie," Tank suggested.

"Okay, let's go into the TV room," I said.

Richie sat next to me on the couch, his arm draped casually across the back of the cushions behind me.

"Richie, about today," I whispered.

"Shh. You don't have to tell me anything," he said.

"But that guy—it was noth—" I tried again.

"It's okay. I just get a little jealous, especially when it comes to you," Richie said.

"Really?" I asked.

"Sara guessed that you didn't sit with us at lunch because you were upset about something. But when you said everything was fine, I just figured . . . Let's just forget about it. Okay?"

"Good idea," I agreed. I settled back against Richie's arm to watch the rest of the movie.

I was still thinking about our talk later when Nell and I were in our beds. A lot of things had changed since Nell had come to visit us. And I was happy that they had. When I looked at Nell, I realized that she was a lot like me. We had grown up so differently but we did have a lot in common after all. I was glad she was my sister.

"Psst, Dani," Nell whispered. "Are you awake?"

"Yes."

"I was just thinking . . ."

"About what?" I asked her.

"About how happy I am right now. Thanks to you. I'm happy that I have my dad, my stepmom, and you."

"Me, too," I said.

"Oh, and Dani?"

"Yes, Nell."

"I need to get up for a minute. I forgot to do something," she said.

"Okay," I said, holding my arm so that my bracelet shimmered against the light. And, just then, Nell flipped off the bathroom light.

About the Author

As a writer of books for young people, CAROL J. PERRY is sometimes invited to speak to school children about writing. One day while she was talking to a group of sixth-graders at Madeira Beach Middle School in Madeira Beach, Florida, Ms. Perry met two girls. They were friends, and they were each named Danielle. That was the incident that sparked the idea for *One Sister Too Many*.

Ms. Perry has written many books for young readers. Some of Ms. Perry's other books published by PAGES Publishing Group include *Tiger Woods: The Making of a World-Class Champion*, *10 Women Political Pioneers*, *13 and Loving It*, and *My Perfect Winter*.

Ms. Perry is always interested in hearing from her readers.